MW00443317

SILENCED

Consent Of The Governed

Book One

B. D. Lutz

ISBN: 978-1-7352793-3-6

Contact the author via email: CLELUTZ11@gmail.com

ACKNOWLEDGEMENTS

I'd like to thank all of my friends and family for their support. And a special thanks to Heidi, Darline, Russ, Aundre, Tim, Charley, and Sean. Without all of your encouragement, this simply doesn't happen.

To the American Military: Without you standing watch over this great nation, this book may not have been possible. You do what few among us have the courage to do. Thank you.

Edited by Monique Happy Editorial Services
www.moniquehappyeditorial.com

Thank you for your hard work and guidance.

Cover designed by: Kelly A. Martin
www.kam.design

Kelly, you are a master at your craft!

Photography by:
funkeyfactory (DepositPhotos), rudi (DepositPhotos), eric1513 (DepositPhotos)

Prologue

6 p.m. Election Night

Jack locked the door to Stinger Machinery, officially ending the best day in company history. The reps from Straus Precision had liked what they'd seen. So much, in fact, that they signed the contract without question. He was still in disbelief. Straus' attorney agreed to his terms without a hint of trepidation. Jack had built in a twenty-percent negotiating cushion and nearly fell over when his new customer inked the deal with only a cursory review.

He craned his neck skyward and smiled, imagining his dad gazing down on him doing the same. He'd be issuing a purchase order for the new CNC Lathe tomorrow morning. It should be sitting in his shop in six months. Stinger Machinery was growing.

He pulled out his phone, ready to dial his wife, Lisa, with the news when it buzzed. She'd beaten him to it.

"Well?" she asked excitedly.

"They signed the flipping thing! No questions asked. Babe, we got the contract, the largest contract in company history!"

The whooping and hollering from the speaker sounded like fun, so he joined her. The excitement and anxiety of the day were released in a celebratory howl.

When their celebration died down, Jack asked, "And well, yourself? What's the word?"

"I'm sorry, Mister Stinger."

Jack's heart sank, instantly forgetting about the day's achievement.

"From now on," Lisa said, "you'll need to refer to me as BYT-Chemical's new Director of Research and Development, Lisa Stinger."

"You got it? You got the promotion!"

"I did. They just made the offer. And I accepted."

"I say we celebrate!" Jack practically screamed into the phone. "We get pizza and watch the election results roll in. We'll save the steak dinner for the weekend. Deal?"

The Stingers were political junkies and never missed an opportunity to vote. They scanned the results like hawks. It had become a tradition for them, one they looked forward to... as long as their candidates and issues won. And this year, their choices had to win.

"Oh, you're so romantic, Jack Stinger. I can only say DEAL! I gotta go. Can't be late for my first meeting as Boss Lady." Lisa hung up as soon as she finished.

Jack sat in his idling Yukon for a long minute, his smile threatening to tear his lips as he shifted into gear and stomped on the gas.

Chapter 1

Inauguration Day

Chief of Staff Roberts watched the reaction of the President's cabinet appointees and guests as the newly sworn-in Commander-in-Chief entered the Oval Office. Those reactions would dictate who he'd grant priority access to... and who would beg for it.

The pecking order was determined quickly. He'd review the video of the event later to ensure he hadn't missed something, but he felt confident his choices would stick.

Thirty minutes later, the handshakes and photo ops wrapped up, and a mountain of executive orders was placed on James Eden's desk.

Roberts stuffed his amusement as Eden's unsteady hand began dismantling the previous administration's legacy. After he signed the initial three orders, the solitary ones Eden had any knowledge of, his sharp-elbowed handlers nearly bum-rushed the press from the Oval Office and killed the video feed.

Eden leaned back in his chair and appeared to doze. So when he spoke, it startled Roberts. "How much longer?" Eden asked, his eyes still closed.

"We have fourteen additional orders to sign and a meeting with our friends from social media," Roberts started. "Then you're off to bed, Mister President."

"Mister President has a nice ring to it," Eden said through his dreadful crooked smile.

"It certainly does, sir. Time to sign the rest of those EOs; we shouldn't keep Jay and Marc waiting."

Like a puppet on a string, Eden leaned forward and put pen to work. With each executive order, singular personal freedoms of the American populace disappeared. It all seemed too easy. *He truly is just a talking head*, Roberts mused as order after order received Eden's signature. The man hadn't read a single word; he literally had no idea what he was signing.

Roberts' spine went stiff as Vice President Sheila Genus' cackling laughter filled the Oval Office. She was the one person Roberts wielded no power over. Her unfettered access to Eden was a necessary evil, one he intended to find a way to manage.

"James! Oh, I'm sorry, Mister President. How does it feel to be helming the most powerful country on the planet?"

"It feels powerful. Yes, powerful is the feeling," Eden sputtered.

Genus' expectant stare went unanswered. "Well, it feels powerful to serve as your second-in-command, sir."

With a flash of his former self, Eden locked eyes with Sheila. "*Second* in command. Remember that, remember your place."

Genus' smile vanished as Eden's statement registered.

Roberts nearly burst into laughter at Eden's declaration. *Neither of you idiots is in control.* The thought forced a smile. The moment passed quickly as Eden's flash of lucidity held longer than Roberts expected.

"What's so funny, Roberts?" Eden said, eyes firmly on his chief of staff.

"Err, nothing, sir, just caught up in the momentous occasion. Your victory was hard-fought, sir, and finally being here makes me happy."

"Yeah, well, you won't be smiling long. We've got hard work ahead of us. The kind you're not used to. So wipe that shit-eating grin off your face, man, and get, um, get... bring those, um. You know who I'm talking about. Bring them in."

Roberts nearly laughed in the man's face. The speed with which Eden's mind clicked in and out of lucidity was astonishing. "Yes, Mister President, I'll have Jay and Marc shown in."

"You do that, Roberts. The President and I have much to discuss with our friends."

Eden's glare bounced to his VP. "*We* aren't talking to them. I am. You'll be leaving with Mister Roberts. As I have already told you, know your place, Genus."

With a nod, Roberts pivoted and exited the Oval Office with the VP in tow. As they entered the adjoining security room, Roberts glanced at Genus and just above a whisper said, "You'll thank him for this." Answering her questioning stare, he said, "Trust me, you don't want to be in that meeting."

CHAPTER 2

SEVEN HOURS POST INAUGURATION CEREMONY

Jay Daisy sat next to Marc Burg in the legendary office. But neither seemed phased by its grandeur. They'd worked tirelessly to win this office for Eden, an achievement for which they expected to be richly compensated.

James Eden shuffled to the couch opposite theirs, practically collapsing into it as he sat. "Gentlemen, the hour's growing late, so I'll be brief."

Jay glanced at his watch. It was seven-thirty post meridian.

"I wanted to thank you both, personally. Your organizations played a pivotal role in this victory. Your dedication to my campaign and our vision for a new America tipped the scales in our favor."

Eden paused, pressing his hand to his right ear. "Oh yes, yes. But our work isn't finished. In fact, it's just beginning. We must curtail the voices of dissent. And it starts with the loudest voice."

"He's going to screw this up. I should be in there with him," Genus hissed at Roberts.

"No," Roberts answered sharply. "He's the only one to have direct contact with them. They've been adamant that they won't speak to anyone but the President."

The two watched anxiously from the security room adjoining the Oval Office. Roberts had a direct line to Eden via audio link to the President's earpiece. The video feed, which Roberts was recording, gave them four unique angles of the office.

Unhappy with Roberts' rebuke, Genus shifted gears. "Why are we moving so quickly? Shouldn't we wait until after the midterms to ensure we hold both the House and Senate?"

"You're thinking in terms of yesteryear's politics, *Madam* Vice President. We have the winning formula; we no longer need to play nice with the other team. In fact, we plan to tear out their throats."

"You will refer to me as Vice President Genus. Madam is an obsolete gendered term."

Roberts didn't respond and let his challenging gaze linger on the VP until she turned away. *Good, you're learning your place!*

Eden's rambling pulled Roberts' attention back to the Oval Office. Due to Genus' endless prattling, the reason behind Eden's sputtering response was lost to him.

"I've already explained, Marc. Apply more pressure on them, all of them. We, um, we're going to, um…" Eden placed his hand to his ear again, then snapped back to his sentence. "Going to run cover. You've no doubt seen the media coverage. The former administration is being dragged through the mud. Everything they touch becomes tarnished. They'll never work in DC again. Every word they utter is fact-checked and labeled as false. We expect you to do the same to their followers. We've done…"

Eden suddenly stopped speaking, eyes focused on some distant memory. Roberts panicked. He recognized what was happening. But Marc Burg interjected before he could shut the conversation down. "Mister President, my team continues to support that effort. We are deplatforming hundreds of people daily. I'm sure Jay's people have been doing the same. However, several of the iconoclasts have filed lawsuits against our fact-checkers, a half-dozen of them to be exact. We've lost each suit brought against us. Our litigation resources are finite."

Marc shifted his gaze to Jay in hopes his counterpart would add credence to his statement. But the man appeared as clueless as Eden. Marc shook his head in disgust and continued his plea. "We need more support with litigation expenses and, more importantly, outcomes."

Eden jumped, surprised by some unseen influence. "Sure, sure, whatever you want, Marc. We're taking action to curtail both. Wait until you hear about the Bureau of Harm Reduction. Man, it's going to be something."

"Sir, don't curtail our funds, only the litigation. Have I been clear? Also, I'd like to hear more about this… what did you call it, Bureau of Harm Reduction?"

Eden's mention of the BHR spurred Roberts to move. He pulled his headset off, cut the video feed, and stormed into the Oval Office. "Gentlemen, the President is calling a lid. I'll see you out."

Eden appeared confused by the intrusion, moving his empty gaze between his guests and Roberts. It seemed as if he didn't recognize his Chief of Staff.

Vice President Genus stepped between Eden and Roberts and called the First Lady into the office. Jan Eden joined the VP at the couch, and together they pulled James from the couch and whisked him away.

**

Roberts escorted their allies through the tunnel exit of the White House, which dumped out near H Street. This would likely be the first of many such walks through the labyrinth of tunnels, which had sat unused for decades. The master plan demanded secrecy, as did the people setting that plan in motion.

"So, tell us more about that bureau Eden mentioned? Specifically, I'd like to know its impact on our organizations." Other than greeting the President, this was the only time Jay had uttered a word.

"Gentlemen, rest assured you and your organizations remain imperative to our success. This administration will move heaven and earth to insulate you from unnecessary oversight. Just make sure your algorithms do as we ask."

Marc caught the nuance in Roberts' phrasing. "Who'll be determining what is necessary and unnecessary?"

"Have faith, Mister Burg. This administration rewards loyalty. Good evening, gentlemen," Roberts said as he shuffled the men into the secured alleyway leading to H Street.

Roberts was dialing a number before the heavy steel door had slammed shut. "Hello, Miss Woods. I have a name to add to your list."

CHAPTER 3

STINGER MACHINERY, EIGHT MONTHS POST INAUGURATION

Jack stormed towards the office area of Stinger Machinery. The call from Jennifer, his receptionist, couldn't have come at a worse time. His lathe went down an hour ago, in the middle of processing the second phase of Straus Precision's order. If he didn't get these crankshafts loaded and shipped by tomorrow morning, Stinger Machinery would lose the contract and probably cease to exist.

The three-month-old, twenty-five-thousand-dollar machine had been rock solid until today. His shop technician, Armin, was struggling to diagnose the problem. Even after an hour on the phone with the manufacturer's tech support, the lathe remained idle.

Out of frustration, Armin had pulled the tool-turret apart, its cutting heads now littering the shop's floor. Jack could literally see the contract evaporating in front of him.

He had asked Jennifer to tell the visitors to leave. Her response sent his blood pressure through the roof. "I'm sorry, Jack. They helped themselves to your office."

Jack's pace quickened with each step. You best be dropping off a check for millions of dollars, he thought as he entered the building's cramped office area, slamming the door to the shop behind him.

He nearly came to a stop when he saw who was waiting for him. The gray suits, dour expressions, and black leather briefcases told him all he needed to know.

"So, to what do I owe the honor of government officials visiting Stinger Machinery?" he asked while taking a seat at his desk.

Unfazed by his brisk greeting, the gray suit seated closest to him spoke. "I'm Agent Amanda Woods. I represent the Bureau of Harm Reduction. My colleague is Agent Cindy Cummings, representing the Bureau of Civic Responsibility. I'm confident I speak for both of us when I say it's a pleasure to meet you."

Jack remained silent as the agent's expectant gaze seemed to hold on him for hours. "I don't like to waste time. You already know my name, you know what I do, and you probably know what I had for lunch. So, Miss Woods, I have a business to run, and your visit is making that impossible. Cut to the chase."

"Please refer to me as Agent Woods. Let's be clear, you inherited this business from your father. Please don't act as if you built it. And I see no reason our visit should be a confrontational encounter. Unless, of course, you're hiding something." A sideways grin broke on the bureaucrat's face. "Do you have something to hide, Jack?"

"Please refer to me as Mister Stinger," Jack shot back. "And, to answer your question, I do not. The visit from the ATF last month was tantamount to a prostate exam. If I was hiding something, the ATF would have found it. I'd tell you to review the ATF's notes, but you already have. So, I'll ask you again, why are you here?"

Agent Woods bristled at Jack's sharp tone. She was accustomed to being feared by commoners, especially ones with something to lose, like Jack Stinger.

With a forced calm, she moved forward. "Mister Stinger, the BHR, in coordination with the BCR, have been tasked with the singular focus of ensuring the safety of the American people. To accomplish this goal, it is our duty to partner with the business community to ensure the products they produce aren't modified in a way that allows them to be used in nefarious or harmful activities."

"Agent Woods, I'll once again refer you to the ATF report. Their agents also arrived unannounced, they too expressed concern for the safety of the American people, and they found nothing to indicate nefarious activity. Every piece of bar stock, every metal billet, everything was counted. They inspected my machines, questioned my employees, and audited my books. Now, if your intent is to perform a similar investigation, you will have free and unobstructed access to my books. However, access to my employees won't be granted until the end of the workday."

Through gritted teeth, Agent Cummings spoke for the first time. "Mister Stinger, I find it troubling that you would mention your inventory. One comprising items easily modified to produce firearms."

Agent Cummings' bookworm appearance had masked a simmering anger towards her political opposites, now she directed it at Jack. Her anger was fine with him; he'd had enough. During the administration's short eight months in power, they had honed the skill of government overreach to a razor's edge. His taxes had nearly tripled, the endless regulations were threatening to cripple his ability to run his family's business, and his raw materials cost had skyrocketed.

"Agent Cummings, aren't you swerving into the ATF's lane? I'm not licensed for firearms manufacturing, nor am I interested in getting that license. Stinger Machinery produces parts for the automobile industry. And only that industry."

Agent Cummings flushed with anger. "All lanes are my lane, Mister Stinger. You'd do well to keep that in mind as our meeting progresses."

Jack's eyebrows hitched. This little mouse has fangs.

"Speaking of your inventory," she said, "according to your Form 85MPR-Material Purchase Record, Stinger Machinery purchased eight hundred linear feet of 416 Stainless Steel two months ago. However, your Form 85PR-Production Record shows your output for that product was seven hundred and ninety-seven feet. Your Form 85WAR-Waste Accounting Record doesn't contain the missing three feet."

Leaning forward, she placed the reports in front of him.

"Is this a joke?" Jack asked, piercing eyes meeting Cummings'. "What are you accusing me of?"

Smug and full of condescension, Cummings replied, "Mister Stinger, why would your first thought be that of accusation? Maybe the government is concerned about your efficiency when working with such an expensive item. Maybe we're here to help."

Jack pinched the bridge of his nose, working hard to stuff his anger. But those words! "So, you're from the government and you're here to help? Well, that makes me feel much better. You should have just said something. If I had known, I would have put my business up for sale. Selling it would be much less painful than watching the government crush it."

Agent Cummings leaned back in her chair and steepled her fingers. "Mister Stinger, your aggressive approach to our conversation, coupled with your inability to complete the mandated resource tracking forms, confirms that our decision to inject Harm Reduction Observers into your organization is the right one."

Jack fought his instinct to launch over his desk and strangled the self-righteous bureaucrat. "Agent Cummings, you'll do nothing of the sort. I've broken no laws. If you'll be so kind as to review my Form 85UI-Unused Inventory, you'll note that Stinger Machinery has accounted for the missing bar stock. I will not tolerate government officials lurking around MY business." Eyes shifting to Agent Woods, he said, "My business, the one my family built. The one I helped grow."

"Mister Stinger," Agent Cummings interrupted, "your Form 85UI-Unused Inventory was filled out incorrectly and received late. Therefore, it will not be entered into record. Those resources are considered missing."

Jack felt the noose tighten around his neck. He was on their radar and would remain there forever. His jaw hinged open to end the meeting.

"Tell us more about Otto?" Woods cut in.

Thrown by the abrupt change in the conversation, Jack paused a moment before answering, "Who?"

"Otto. Oh, what's his last name? Oh, yes, Otto Hammer. Tell us more about Otto Hammer."

Jack's gut clenched. "Are you referring to the main character in my book? The zombie book I wrote?"

The slimy smile on Woods' face answered Jack's question before she spoke. "I am. Actually, we're both curious to hear more about him."

Jack clung to his razor-thin shred of patience, taking a deep breath in hopes it would take the edge off. It didn't. "Why in the hell are you asking me about my book? A book that is no longer available to purchase because it offended some thin-skinned bureaucrat sitting in her ivory tower in DC? A book I wrote as a bucket list item after my parents were killed last year. What in the actual hell does it have to do with my business?"

Sharing a knowing glance with her counterpart, Woods turned back to Jack and said, "Well, Mister Stinger, the book was quite critical of several politicians, actually an entire political party. We're working to unify America, and your book was anything but unifying. So, I'm sure you understand our concern."

Jack stared, unbelieving, at Woods, worry seeping into his mind. "The book was about ZOMBIES, for Christ's sake. You know, monsters that eat people. You understand it's fiction, right? And my political views are my business. The last I checked, the Constitution guaranteed me the right to voice them freely." Jack's head swiveled between the two government bulldogs before he continued. "Do you have anything else? Because I have a business to run, something I'm guessing neither of you understands."

Woods leaned in close, reveling in her achievement of rattling the man. "Mister Stinger, I'm sure you're familiar with the saying 'Write what you know'."

Chapter 4

Friend Me's World Headquarters

Marc Burg paced the length of his office as sweat poured down his back. Friend Me's world headquarters had transformed into a sweltering hell. One which he now believed he would never escape.

"Mister Roberts, our power consumption is well below government mandate. We take climate change seriously at Friend Me. Should I list the steps we've taken to ensure the planet is a better place for our next generation?"

"No need, Marc. I'm sure your conservation efforts are commendable. But your Form 85EC-Energy Consumption Reports don't lie. That monstrosity of a building is simply using too much energy." Roberts couldn't help but smile at Burg's distress. "May I ask, why on earth have you chosen to bother me regarding the condition of your thermometer? This situation clearly calls for intervention by the Bureau of Energy Equality. Or possibly the Bureau of Energy Consumption would be more helpful. I might even suggest trying the Bureau of Power Supply."

Marc ran a sweaty palm over his slick face. "You know why I'm talking to you, Roberts! I want your Harm Reduction Observers out of my damn building. My loyalty to Eden's administration has been unwavering. I see no reason for the intrusion. Cutting off access to my building's HVAC system seems a punishment for my request to have them removed."

Drunk on power, Roberts rose to his feet. He'd been waiting for this moment, and his mouth watered with anticipation. "Marc, do you have something to hide? If you want to confess, we can grant you immunity under the Whistleblower Act." He nearly burst into laughter when he heard Burg's sharp inhale. "I take it you don't, so the Observers will remain until such time as we determine we can fully trust Friend Me. Your air-conditioning privileges will be reinstated after our Observers report their findings. And, after you complete the Form 85ECRR-Energy Consumption Reinstatement Request, of course."

"TRUST ME! You must be joking. Friend Me has been loyal to this administration from day one. Even in the face of countless congressional probes, we held fast to the ideals of James' vision. The only reason I'm on the phone with you is because the man for whom I risked Friend Me's very existence won't take my calls. My organization has nothing to hide, and I certainly don't require the protection of the Whistleblower Act."

Roberts cut Marc's tirade off. "You posed a question to me after your meeting in the Oval Office. Do you recall your question, Mister Burg? Don't bother answering. I'll refresh your memory. You asked who determines necessary oversight. To answer your question: I do, Mister Burg. I determine necessary oversight. And our oversight of the world's largest, most influential social media platform is very necessary. And it will remain in place until you do as we've directed and eliminate opposition exposure on your platform."

Burg went cold; this was how Nazi Germany operated. Control the information and you control the message. Control the message and yours is the only truth.

"Now, Marc, Friend Me will have all opposing news outlets deplatformed by day's end. They're feeding misinformation to domestic terrorists, and we can't give them a voice. It's for the safety of our fellow Americans. Do your civic duty, or we'll do it for you. Have I been clear?"

Burg recognized what Roberts was saying. And the realization that he no longer controlled the company he'd built threatened to crush him. "Crystal, Mister Roberts. You've been crystal clear."

Roberts loved this part. Destroying capitalists was quickly becoming his drug of choice. "Good to hear. Submit your Form 85ECRR-Energy Consumption Reinstatement Request directly to me. I'll expedite it and get your air conditioning back online; we can't have those beautiful servers overheating. Consider it a bone from your master."

Burg stood staring at the blazing California sun through the wall of windows bordering his office, his government-issued cell phone clutched in his hand. "Tell our team to remove them, deplatform every single one of them. Every news outlet, advertiser, and individual user gets shut down. If they so much as supported a single policy of the previous administration, deplatform them."

Alana wiped a tear from her eye. She had heard the entire call and knew what it meant. "I'll make the call to our moderators now." She tried to make eye contact with Marc, but his head remained bowed. "Can we stop them?"

Marc simply shook his head.

***

Roberts leaned back in his chair, letting his buzz wash over him. He was the second most powerful person in America, and he loved it.

His bliss snapped when his personal cell phone chirped, the unique ringtone leaving no doubt who was calling. "Mister Rosos, I've been awaiting your call. I'm pleased to inform you that everything is on schedule."

Roberts went silent, listening intently to Rosos. "Yes sir, I have my pen in hand. Please continue." He scribbled furiously, trying to keep pace with Rosos' rapid-fire dictation. He'd learned early that his keeper expected perfect execution. He was tempted to request that Mister Rosos transmit his instructions via email or their encrypted messenger app. But he bit his tongue. The verbal beating he'd endured when he'd made the mistake of asking for emailed instructions two years ago remained a fresh wound. And he was too close to the prize to have Rosos scuttle his career.

"Mister Rosos, I'll act on your directives immediately. Phase two commences today."

CHAPTER 5

THE PENTAGON

Major General Adam Stein read the directive for the third time. The words hadn't changed. He glanced at the wall in his office, the one which told the story of his service to the United States.

Stein had graduated from West Point in 1990, then deployed to the Middle East sandbox and lived in the gritty shit-hole non-stop during his first ten years of service. He'd lost soldiers, took the lives of countless enemy combatants, and witnessed the worst of mankind. But this directive shook him to his core. In the middle of his wall of memories was the Oath of Commissioned Officers, one line standing out among the rest: "I will support and defend the Constitution of the United States against all enemies, foreign and domestic; that I will bear true faith and allegiance to the same."

He held in his trembling hand the greatest challenge to his oath. "Enemies foreign and domestic," he mumbled as he sorted through the directive's true meaning.

His cell buzzed, jolting him from his fear-induced daze. "Chairman Alderson, I'm assuming you received the directive from Eden," he said, sans military formality.

"General Stein," Alderson responded, "I have reviewed the directive. I was also fortunate enough to receive a call from Chief of Staff Roberts. He cautioned me that disobeying a direct order from the President is an Article-92 offense. He then reminded me of the ramifications of being found guilty by a military tribunal. I've tried to reach Eden, but he's still not taking my calls."

"Sir, this directive, this order, isn't lawful. I can't, in good conscience, enact it," Stein protested.

"Stein, you can, and you will. The directive specifically states that President Eden sees a clear and present danger posed by a contingent of rogue military service members loyal to the previous administration. As Director of Manpower and Personnel, you will do as directed."

"Where's the proof, the intelligence, confirming his fears? I've seen nothing to support that accusation."

The words next spoken nearly stopped his heart. "They'll manufacture it. I'm not losing my pension over this. Start the review process today."

Stein placed his phone carefully on his desk. He'd anticipated budget cuts and slanderous news headlines. But he'd never anticipated this move. Eden was aiming to cripple the military. His directive would transform the military into a worthless husk, a shell.

Stein pulled his personal cell from his breast pocket. He was in no mood to allow Eden's gray suits to listen to his personal calls via his newly issued government cell. Considering the conversation he'd just had while using it, he was probably already on their watch list. He thumbed through his contacts list until he found the number for his friend and former mentor. He needed the man's guidance. But mostly, he needed to vent.

"So, how's retired life treating you? Getting fat, or are you still futzing around that withered jumble of weeds you call a garden?"

"General, I'm sorry, Major General Stein. I woke up this morning with a bad feeling, and now I know why." His friend laughed as he spoke. "Christ, tell me you're not planning on visiting me! The fishing's good on Lake Erie this time of year, but I'd probably end up tossing you overboard."

Stein, as serious as a heart attack, said, "Well, Colonel, I've been asked to contact you regarding your Form 85VRP-Vital Recourse Production. Seems you failed to submit it to the proper authorities prior to cultivating your land. Our gray suits will be paying you a visit later this afternoon."

After a long silence, his friend asked, "Is this your gov-issued cell?"

"I'm always on it, especially when conducting official government business." A mischievous smile curled his lips.

"Good, tell Eden he can kiss my ass. And tell your gray suits that I may be old, but I can still pull a trigger!"

The long-time friends shared a lengthy and much-needed laugh, but when it stopped Stein's mood darkened. "Do you have ten minutes? I really need to talk."

***

When the call ended, Stein knew what he needed to do. His friend had predicted this, spouting off about the corrupting lure of absolute power. He had called him crazy, but now he wasn't sure.

"Miss Jones," he barked from his desk, "I need every commanding officer on a secured line by tomorrow afternoon."

Chapter 6

Stinger Machinery

Jack leaned against his Yukon's grill, staring at his building while sipping piping hot coffee from his travel mug. This place held so many memories. Jack had spent every day after school here, waiting for his mom to pick him up on her way home from the hospital where she worked as a nurse. He could still hear his dad yelling at his seven-year-old self to leave the machinists alone. How'd that go? *Unless you're ready to run one of those machines, you best find your ass a seat in the office. Pronto!*

The place was much smaller back then. The addition he'd added after his dad passed almost tripled its footprint and nearly bankrupted him. But it'd been paying dividends ever since.

He kept the original structure intact, unable to see it razed to make way for the new building. His Uncle Willis seemed disproportionately happy with that decision. *Too many memories in that building to tear it down*, he'd told Jack. He'd converted it to their much-needed office space. Jack learned quickly that growing the business meant more than simply expanding Stinger Machinery's production capabilities.

The offices now housed a substantial sales force, a human resources manager, and a full-time accountant. He'd been outsourcing the latter two positions until last year. Stinger Machinery was becoming a major industry player.

"*Was* being the key word," Jack said while sipping his coffee. He'd been resisting the BHR's attempts to inject their bulldogs into his business. Several heated phone calls culminated with two gray suits arriving unannounced yesterday. He'd refused to allow them to enter, turning them away before they'd made it to the building's front door.

Today, bright red spray paint covered the building. The graffiti boldly proclaimed Jack a racist, capitalist pig.

"Well, they got the capitalist part right." The voice belonged to Armin, and it nearly scared Jack out of his skin.

He pivoted to face Stinger Machinery's long-time shop technician, and Jack's right hand man. He recognized the look on the man's dark features. Armin was angry.

"Why the hell would they do this, Jack? I mean, we both expected them to turn up the heat after yesterday. But this, it's just intimidation. They're trying to bully you into submission, bully us."

"Armin, things are changing quickly. The BHR and BCR are the equivalent to Nazi Brownshirts. Our Friend Me and Chirp accounts have vanished as well. I checked them this morning, and they're gone. No error message, no technical issues, and no temporary suspension notice. They're gone. No trace of them. I'm afraid…"

Jack's phone buzzed, cutting him off. "Where are you guys? I called over an hour ago," he said, assuming it was the police department responding to his early morning call about the vandalism.

"*Mister* Stinger. I received word of a terrible act of vandalism to your building. I certainly hope no one was injured. How can I help?"

Jack flushed with anger but realized that raging at Agent Woods would only escalate the situation. He wasn't taking her bait. "Agent Woods, I appreciate your concern, but we have things under control." He paused, understanding taking over. "I'd appreciate it if you would allow the local police to respond. I need a police report for insurance."

"Oh, *Mister* Stinger, I'm sure you do. But it seems the local police are busy tending to other, more pressing matters. However, I have a solution. BHR Observers have authorization to complete the Form 85CIR-Criminal Incident Report documents you'll need to submit your claim. I'll dispatch them to your location."

"No! I'll handle it myself," Jack barked. "No need to bother your team. I'm sure they're busy fighting the good fight for our country." He nearly gagged on his words.

"*Mister* Stinger, it appears your business has become a target for local hooligans. Considering the importance of the products Stinger Machinery produces, I'm afraid I must insist that our Observers integrate into your organization. They'll arrive within the hour. Please be sure to sign the Form 85OI-Observer Integration. It'll allow us to withdraw funds—from your bank—to pay the salary of the BHR employees assigned to Stinger Machinery. Providing harm reduction is an expensive endeavor."

Jack's vision went red. They were going to smother him in bureaucratic paperwork, break his financial back, and then make a move for his business. He pushed away from the hood of his Yukon and walked in a circle, trying to bleed off his anger.

Forcing the edge from his voice, he said, "I'll fix the damage myself. Have a painting party for my team, cook hotdogs, play music, treat it like a company outing. It'll be an excellent opportunity for some team building. I'll hire a security company to watch the place at night. No need to involve the government. Unless you can have my social media accounts restored, that is."

After a long pause, Agent Woods spoke. "Very well. However, a daily fine of two thousand dollars will be levied against your business."

"For what?" Jack shouted.

"*Mister* Stinger, the government has strict rules surrounding Optic Litter Control. Your building is now an eyesore, a blight, if I may. It'll take several days to secure the proper permit from your local government and, as you know, work can't begin until you complete and submit your Form 85EPR-Exterior Property Repair, which I'll mail sometime next week. In light of the added expense, you should reconsider performing the repairs yourself."

"I own this property. Applying a fresh coat of paint shouldn't involve... you know what. I'll do it myself. Fine me all you want. Now, I have to get to work. Good day, Agent Woods."

"*Mister* Stinger. One more thing. I'm sorry to hear about the Straus contract. We'll talk soon."

Jack's gut clenched. Woods had delivered a deathblow. He turned to face Armin, who was staring wide-eyed at him. "What, Jack? What happened?"

"I need to call Straus."

***

Jack sat at his desk, ignoring the worried stares of his employees gathered outside his office door. He couldn't wrap his mind around it. *It's got to be more than my book! What put me on their radar?*

Armin cleared his throat, pulling Jack's attention to his team. Their future hung in the balance, and his delay in sharing the information was the equivalent of death by fire ants. He stood and walked into the main office area to face them.

"If you haven't noticed, I did something to someone, and we're paying the price for it. Straus Precision is suspending its order indefinitely."

His accountant's voice rose above the shocked gasps of his team. "Jack, they can't do that. We have a contract. We've dedicated nearly seventy percent of our production capabilities to them. It'll bankrupt us!"

Jack struggled to find the words to counter Alison Abrams' statement. But her assessment was accurate; it *would* bankrupt them. In a matter of weeks, Stinger Machinery would be forced to close its doors. He returned the stunned and frightened gaze of his employees. They believed in this company; their futures depended on his next move.

"To answer your question, Alison, Straus received a call from the Bureau of Government Acquisition informing them that they—they being our government—may purchase a vehicle from Straus at some point in the future. But because of their relationship with Stinger Machinery, the government would decline the opportunity to purchase Straus products."

Armin exploded, "That's bullshit, Jack. Straus fabricates high-performance, specialty vehicles. The government has no reason to buy anything Straus produces. Not a single damn thing! This is intimidation. They're acting like the Mafia. I say screw them! We've made it through tougher times; we'll make it again."

Jack caught Armin's phrasing: "We." This was more than the threat of losing a job for Armin; it was his family being threatened. He smiled at his friend, knowing Armin meant it. He'd walk away from the contract in a second. But Armin didn't speak for everyone; these people had families to feed.

"Armin, I agree," Jack started. "But for Straus it was more about why the government blackballed Stinger and less about lost sales."

Jack's focus was broken by technical manuals slamming onto a desk from the back of the office, pulling everyone's attention to Randy Munson. The mountain of a man looked angry, and Jack cursed himself for not including him.

Randy had joined Stinger seventeen years earlier and was a master machinist. Deaf since birth, Randy had struggled to get a job doing what he loved: working with metal. After being hired at Stinger, communication quickly became a challenge which led to some very costly mistakes. Randy grew frustrated and came to Jack's father to submit his resignation.

Jack's father refused to accept it. Instead, he made a deal with Randy. He and the other employees, including Jack, who was just cutting his teeth at managing Stinger Machinery, would take classes to learn sign language. After they learned the basics, if Randy still wanted to leave, he obviously couldn't stop him. But Jack's dad recognized the raw talent Randy possessed and knew he was an asset. He was willing to try anything to keep him.

From that day forward, every new hire at Stinger was required to learn sign language.

But right now, Randy was extremely aggravated. He had no idea what was happening; he only saw the worried faces of his co-workers gathered for an impromptu meeting.

Jack signed to Randy, "I'm sorry, my friend." He shifted his gaze to Armin and asked, "Can you bring Randy up to speed? I need to make a call."

CHAPTER 7

THE BUREAU OF HARM REDUCTION

Chief of Staff Roberts approached the offices of the Bureau of Harm Reduction. The unassuming door, tucked away on the fifth floor of the Eisenhower Executive Office Building, held no plaque or insignia identifying who or what was behind it.

This unannounced visit would be Roberts' first to the BHR office. It was a purposeful visit. Just to remind them that he was always watching the watchers.

Roberts stopped at the entrance, imagining the scene on the other side. A vision of an old man resembling a bespectacled Crypt Keeper, perched behind a desk piled high with files, brought a smirk to his face. *I watched too much television growing up.*

As his hand touched the knob, his phone buzzed. It was Press Secretary Regina Scarlet, again.

"Regina?"

A pause ensued as Regina waited, expecting more from Roberts than simply saying her name.

"Regina, I don't have the time or patience to deal with you. So, quickly, what do you want?"

Through gritted teeth, the Press Secretary responded, "When will Eden be available for a press conference? I'm receiving a lot of pressure, and justifiably so, from the White

House Press Corps. And frankly, Eden needs to get in front of them and the American people. The man hasn't uttered a word in public for months."

"Not true. He spoke last week while boarding Marine One," Roberts countered.

"Waving to reporters and mumbling about his dog doesn't qualify as speaking to the American people, and you know it. Eden must get in front of a camera, a crowd, something for God's sake. He's the leader of the free world, and right now he's AWOL!" Regina shot back.

"Yes, yes, we'll arrange something soonest. Until then, continue to speak the truth. Eden is very busy cleaning up the mess left by the former administration. He's righting the wrongs of those that came before him. He's building a better America."

"Roberts, you know that's a lie. The press wants an explanation about his trade deal with China. The one that seems grotesquely lopsided in China's favor, the agreement that has already eliminated thousands of American jobs. I'd ask the President myself, but he refuses to speak with me. Actually, you and Vice President Genus are the only people with access to him. That needs to change."

Roberts made a quick mental note before responding. "Miss Scarlet, it would be prudent of you to check your tone and stuff your *reporter's* instinct. Career longevity is a rare commodity for unelected officials in DC. History is littered with the carcasses of idealistic youngsters who ran afoul of their superiors. Their keepers, if you will. Follow orders, or that trash heap will grow by one. Have I been clear, Regina?" Roberts ended the call before receiving the Press Secretary's response. He assumed her compliance.

Refocusing his attention on the matter at hand, he grabbed the doorknob and pushed, planning on making a grand entrance into the realm of the BHR. He nearly slammed his face against the heavy oak slab when it refused to budge. Unaccustomed to being denied entry to any office in DC, his anger flared, and he pounded on the heavy oak.

When nothing happened, he searched the area for the telltale signs of video surveillance. He found none. His anger growing, he again pounded on the door and barked a command to be given access. His anger gave way to suspicion. This was a stalling tactic, he surmised. Buying time the BHR staff undoubtedly needed to hide incriminating evidence.

Again he pounded on the door, his mind searching for his next move, when suddenly a voice, seemingly emanating from the heavens, directed him to use his keycard.

"Thank you for pointing out the obvious. But I see no security apparatus to swipe said keycard through," Roberts barked.

"Mister Roberts, you can wave it in front of the knob," the voice countered.

Flustered, Roberts pulled the lanyard from his neck and waved it angrily over the knob, causing the door to emit a chirp and open.

He pushed into the office, expecting to see hordes of BHR staffers scurrying from desk to desk, exchanging data and intelligence under the watchful eye of the Crypt Keeper. Instead, under a blinding array of florescent lighting, he found dozens of enormous computer servers connected to an equal number of output terminals. Above each machine hung a sign identifying them as Bureau of Harm Reduction assignment terminals.

A never-ending line of dead-eyed men and women, wearing the BHR's customary gray suits, stood in pin-straight lines, awaiting their turn at the terminals. The machines spat paper at a frenetic pace into the waiting hands of the BHR staff. As they received their assignments, the gray suits quickly disappeared to the back of the room. *How very Orwellian*, Roberts mused.

Standing on tiptoes, Roberts attempted to gain an unobstructed view of where the dead-eyes scurried to. A football field's length away and barely visible from this distance was an enormous room housing hundreds of '50s-era metal desks, set in the same pin-straight lines the staffers had formed at the terminals, and void of personal effects. A BHR agent occupied each desk, staring blankly at the terminal resting atop the ancient office furniture.

They remained seated until another agent, carrying a fresh assignment, arrived. At that point, the seated person surrendered the desk to the arriving agent. Where they went after that was a mystery, one which he intended to solve.

"Can I help you, Chief of Staff Roberts?" a voice to his right asked.

Startled, Roberts snapped in the voice's direction. *Holy shit, the Crypt Keeper does run this place.* The thought forced a chuckle. Roberts faced a man of roughly eighty years old, sporting a wispy comb-over and eyeglasses whose thickness rivaled that of a magnifying glass. His gaze shifted to the area behind the creepy senior citizen.

A wall of offices appeared to stretch on forever, each void of a door. It dawned on Roberts that the BHR had expanded to where it now occupied the entire fifth floor of the Eisenhower Executive Building. He was unsure if the development was acceptable. Then he smiled inward; of course it was acceptable. He controlled this machine.

Addressing the Crypt Keeper's initial question, Roberts simply nodded and told him to remain seated—not that the old codger was in a rush to escort him anywhere—and began his visit in earnest.

He walked quickly past each office, slowing enough at each entrance for the inhabitant to notice him. More importantly, to notice what his visit meant. Much to his surprise, none seemed intimidated. In fact, they were downright indifferent to his presence.

He rounded the corner and found another equally long row of offices, with doors and name plaques indentifying to whom the office belonged. He was greeted by the same indifference as displayed by what he assumed were the lower-ranking members of the BHR occupying the offices he'd just walked past.

Feeling eyes on him, he turned sharply and found the Crypt Keeper staring at him. "I told you I'm capable of seeing myself about the office. Please return to your station."

Unfazed, the octogenarian smiled and said, "Mister Roberts, if you tell me the name of the person you want to meet with, I can escort you to the correct office. This is an expansive workplace, one you'll be touring for hours without proper directions."

Flustered by the Crypt Keeper and the lack of the expected response from the BHR staff, Roberts blurted out, "Woods. I'm looking for Agent Woods."

"Ah, you're in luck. Agent Woods' office is three doors down, on the right. She's in today but appears busy at the moment. Can I offer you a seat in the waiting area and some cold water?"

"She'll make time for me, of that, I assure you," Roberts countered as he spun to continue his journey.

Finding Woods' office ten steps later, he stood in front of her door and turned to see the Crypt Keeper hadn't moved. Shaking his head, he pushed into Woods' office as she was placing her desk phone into its cradle.

CHAPTER 8

THE BUREAU OF HARM REDUCTION— AGENT WOODS' OFFICE

Agent Woods glanced at Roberts as he entered her office and forced a smile. "Chief of Staff Roberts, it's a pleasure to see you. How may I help you?"

Thrown by her calm, Roberts stumbled through his response. "Agent Woods. This is… um, a quick visit to check on our troops, so to speak." Recovering, Roberts moved to rattle the agent. "I would, however, like an update on the special cases I've assigned to you."

"Of course. I can say, to date, things are progressing nicely." Woods pulled keys from her breast pocket and unlocked a drawer in her desk, out of Roberts' sight.

A moment later, a large stack of folders sat atop her desk. Roberts' eyes bulged as competing thoughts struck him simultaneously: He didn't have the time for a full rundown of the entire stack of files. Moreover, the number of special investigations he had requested was dramatically larger than he realized. And Agent Woods didn't so much as flinch at his accusatory tone.

"Tell you what, Agent Woods. I'll take your word for it that everything is moving along as planned." He paused, organizing his thoughts, then continued. "I have one question which needs an answer. What is the total operational capacity of the BHR?"

Agent Woods removed the files, placing them back under lock and key. "Our capacity is unlimited as long as our budget meets the demand. We've become quite creative with generating revenue. But the threat is ever-present. To answer your question: For current capacity, we're three thousand strong, with daily adds of several hundred. There's no shortage of unemployed persons willing to serve their country."

"I don't recall being briefed on the exponential growth of the Bureau of Harm Reduction. An oversight which I'm confident you'll rectify going forward." Roberts was growing uneasy. He couldn't finger the cause, but it nibbled at his feeling of being in control of the BHR.

"Sir, each of our Form 85SR-Status Reports was forwarded to your office, delivered in person, to your staff, within the mandated submittal dates. I can produce the signed acknowledgments of receipt," Woods proffered.

"Ah yes, I recall seeing several of them," Roberts lied. "But I must admit, I'm falling behind in my administrative duties. Getting America back on track is a time-consuming endeavor. I am curious about our social media strategy. Can you brief me on our progress with Chirp and Friend Me?"

A smile creased Woods' face, the likes of which spoke to her embrace of the power she wielded. "Our agents, in conjunction with agents from the Bureau of Civic Responsibility, have been injected into both organizations. Some they know about, others they don't. I've been working on a progress report but can certainly deliver it verbally right now if you'd prefer?"

Roberts' uneasiness grew. "I'll take the Cliff Notes version."

"Of course, sir. We've melded into both organizations with very little opposition. The pockets of resistance encountered by our operatives were eliminated. Our agents have assumed roles throughout the subject organizations; again some they know about, others they don't. Our visually obvious agents are skillful at being seen, drawing attention away from our embedded assets. We've mined a substantial amount of political opposition data. And we can confirm that both organizations deplatformed every single radical. Not one of them remain an active user."

A rare smile broke on Roberts' face. "Excellent! Agent Woods, tell me. How are your local efforts progressing?"

It was Woods' turn to smile. "Sir, they couldn't be better. The self-proclaimed patriots are putty. Easy to manipulate into any form we desire. Actually, I was just finishing a call with one of our more resistant *patriots* as you entered. I may be enjoying our local engagements a little too much. However, watching them crumble under the full weight of the Federal Government as they spout off about the Constitution, their rights, and whatever other baseless defense they grasp at is extremely gratifying. Especially when I remind myself of the threat they pose to our country. I've enjoyed it to such an extent that I've conducted many of our local level actions myself. And supervise the others."

Something in her delivery rattled Roberts. He should have been encouraged by her commitment, but he wasn't. Someone with a singular focus, such as Woods possessed, could easily lose sight of the overarching goal. Become so vested that when the need for her services diminished, she would become disillusioned, purposeless, and easily swayed by forces promising her the opportunity to continue doing what she loved.

Opposition forces offering her the chance to continue persecuting people they'd convinced her of being her enemy, or an enemy of any cause they championed, could convert her and set her loose on *him*. He made a mental note to keep an eye on this woman.

Roberts' thought broke when his phone buzzed. Looking at the display, he cringed when he saw Regina Scarlet's name. Before answering, he locked Woods in a hard stare and said, "I have an addition for your list."

***

As Roberts exited the Eisenhower, he pushed the send button. "Yes, Agent Cummings. I'd like to add a name to your list."

CHAPTER 9

NINE MONTHS POST INAUGURATION, WILLIS STINGER'S HOME

Jack slammed the Yukon into Park and hurriedly exited his SUV. He was late, and his uncle would be pacing the floor, fit to be tied. Uncle Willis was a punctuality stickler. Even the five minutes Jack was late would drive his uncle crazy.

As he walked towards the door, he pressed the hatch release button on his key fob, hoping to impart the impression of *acceptable time management*. He dared a glance at the picture window and met his uncle's disapproving stare. Jack smiled and waved, receiving a stiff nod in reply. *Shit, he's pissed.* Jack's thought broke when the door suddenly swung open.

"I almost left without you. I considered leaving you a note to join me whenever you decided to show up. Then I speculated that *he may never arrive,* or *Jack may be experiencing car trouble. Maybe he's been involved in a terrible accident.* I was left to wonder what had happened because I received no phone call advising me of your adjusted ETA. I contemplated calling you but reconsidered in fear I might interrupt an EMT working to save your life on the roadside." A wry smile bent the corners of his mouth. "But when you pulled into my driveway, alive and well, I felt great joy and relief, replaced quickly by disappointment in your poor time management skills. However, we may salvage the day if we move, double-quick."

"Good to see you too, UW. We could already be on the lake casting our lines if not for your speech. One of your better ones, I might add."

His uncle stepped out and wrapped Jack in his arms. "Good to see you; we need to do this more often," he said as he pulled away. "Okay, let's go before all the big ones are caught."

Jack looked forward to his fishing trips with his uncle. They'd been doing it since Jack was a runt and UW was home on military leave. He didn't like to fish, but he loved the time spent with his uncle, who now represented the last of Jack's living family.

The frequency of their trips tapered off over the years. Life has a knack for getting in the way of living. But he realized one day the trips would end, and the thought pummeled his emotions. He'd never be ready to be the last living Stinger.

***

As they pulled out of his driveway, Jack took in the neighborhood. "Why did you stay here? You could have moved anywhere you wanted."

Uncle Willis lived in the Tremont area of Cleveland. He'd owned the house for as long as Jack could remember. For years he'd rented it out while serving in the Marines. Being a colonel meant he wasn't home much. But when he was, he'd check on the house and, depending on the season, get Jack out on his boat or behind a rifle hunting deer.

After UW retired, he worked at Stinger Machinery for a couple of years to keep busy. Then one day, he'd decided it was time to dedicate his life to fishing, hunting, and complaining about the government. All of which he excelled at.

"Cleveland is home, Jack. That's why I kept the house. I have no desire for all the trappings money brings. I've got what I need. And, one day, you'll understand why I kept it. Besides, now that Tremont's a social hot spot, it's tripled in value."

Jack felt the message about *understanding* why he kept it was cryptic. But he let the moment pass, concentrating instead on getting them to Edgewater Marina as quickly as possible and in one piece.

The short ride to the marina held the usual conversation, but Jack was distant, mind on the matters at his shop.

"When we get on the lake, you're going to tell me what's on your mind, Jack. You've already thrown a wrench in our timing. I won't let you ruin the entire day by sulking around."

"Not until we're on the lake?" Jack questioned. He knew his uncle; the man never misspoke. Every word had a purpose, sometimes even when he was busting chops.

"Yes, Jack. Not until we're on the lake. Until then, what do you think about the Tribe's chances?"

Jack caught the edge in his uncle's voice and followed his lead. "Well, I'm surprised they're doing as good as they are considering the fire sale after last season. But they've got a snowball's chance in hell of winning the pennant, so forget about the series."

Jack noticed his uncle concentrating on something in his side-view mirror. But without missing a beat, he said, "Yeah, that's what I figured."

The rest of the ride was quiet, and his uncle never took his eyes off the mirror. "When we're on the lake, I have a question or two for you too," Jack said.

UW gave a crooked smile and a stiff nod but remained silent.

CHAPTER 10

CHIEF OF STAFF ROBERTS' OFFICE

Roberts anxiously awaited Rosos' return call. He needed guidance, a plan to divert attention away from Eden's absence. The brief video clips and sound bites released on the White House channel had bought them some time. But the calls for a press conference and, more importantly, a State of The Union address had grown deafening.

Sending Vice President Genus in Eden's stead was unacceptable. Her face already filled every news feed in the country, trying to shift focus away from Eden and relay a sense of normalcy to the American people.

But the President's mental acuity was unpredictable. The situation was growing dire. His cognitive decline was accelerating more quickly than predicted by Rosos' personal doctors. The amounts of daily medications the man received were alarming. And worse, the regimen wasn't working. They needed a few more months.

His phone finally buzzed, and he pulled a deep breath before answering. "Mister Rosos, thank you for returning my call on such short notice. I'm afraid we have a *situation* brewing."

Roberts launched into detailing the problems faced by the administration. And he quickly learned that Rosos shared his concerns. True to form, he already had a solution in mind.

***

Roberts disconnected his call after receiving the lengthy list of action items. His keeper's strategy was beautifully simple. With list in hand, he marched from his office en route to the Press Secretary's office.

On his way, he called the Bureau of Government Security. "Secretary Napoli, I'm calling to inform you of a credible threat received by the White House this morning."

Surprised by Roberts' call, as she'd just been handed the report of the threat, Napoli stumbled through her response. "Sir, I was made aware of the threat as your call came through. Have you secured Eden in the Presidential Emergency Operation Center?"

Roberts smiled. Rosos moved like lightning and had already delivered the *reported* threat to the intelligence community. "No, but he will be secured momentarily. The reason for my call is to gather any additional information you have. Can you clarify anything? The press will demand answers."

"Sir, all I know is that a fringe group of violent domestic terrorists is planning a full assault on the White House and possibly the Capitol. My team feels this is a credible threat posing a clear and present danger to the safety of President Eden and Vice President Genus. Sir, get them to the PEOC immediately. I'm notifying the Secret Service and Capitol Police now. We'll have the area cordoned off in twenty."

The Chief of Staff wasn't satisfied. The threat needed to be met with a stronger response. "Lock down the entire area surrounding the White House. I want roadblocks with police and military presence from Lafayette Square to the Ellipse. Make similar arrangements for the Capitol Building. This is a very credible threat. We must show force."

Roberts disconnected the call, the buzz of power taking hold. He burst into Press Secretary Scarlet's office and instantaneously addressed her stunned expression. "President Eden is being moved to the PEOC. Our assumption is that the previous administration has conspired with violent extremists to overthrow our government. Prepare a press release. Advise the American people that Eden is safe. He will remain under heavy guard until we neutralize the threat. Let them know we will root out every single person responsible, and they will be dealt with accordingly."

As he finished speaking, an alarm sounded throughout the White House. Press Secretary Scarlet scrambled to her feet, fear and confusion straining her pale complexion. Pivoting to face Roberts, she screamed, "What's happening?"

Fighting to contain his smile, he simply shrugged his shoulders and said, "President Eden will be unable to hold a press conference for the foreseeable future."

CHAPTER 11

WILLIS STINGER'S BOAT, LAKE ERIE

The early afternoon sun warmed Jack's face as he tossed his empty beer bottle into the trash and grabbed his third from the cooler. The stress of the last two weeks ebbed as he twisted the cap from the sweating bottle. The sun felt good. It had been a mild November, so mild, in fact, that he had to remind himself that Thanksgiving was only a couple weeks week away.

UW's boat was larger than Jack's first apartment. The fifty-one-foot well-appointed Carver C52 felt like a luxury resort anchored ten miles off Lake Erie's shore. The men had cast their lines from the hydraulic swim platform, making small talk and catching up. But the conversation tapered off as they enjoyed the calm that comes with being near the water.

It hadn't escaped Jack's notice that UW kept glancing towards the shore. It made him uneasy, and when he caught UW doing it for the umpteenth time, he called him on it. "What's got your attention on shore? The action's out here, on the lake."

UW smiled as he stood. "Action? The only action is your empties hitting the trash. We haven't had so much as a nibble. We probably missed the walleye by five minutes."

UW walked toward the galley. As he passed Jack, the younger Stinger was reminded of how imposing the retired Marine was. At six feet, he moved his muscular two-hundred-pound frame like a man half his age. His gray hair, cut into a high and tight, and abundance of worry lines were the only tells of his sixty-two years on earth.

Jack brought the ice-cold Great Lakes IPA to his lips just as his uncle asked him to join him. Pulling a quick gulp from the bottle, he quickly stood and headed towards the galley. Galley was the proper term, but Jack considered it a full-blown kitchen. The area sported every modern amenity available in a house, a nice house.

He found his uncle leaning against the granite countertop. UW's expression was hard, and his eyes drilled into Jack's with an intensity he'd never witnessed from his uncle.

"So, what's on your mind?" UW asked while flipping on the boat-wide stereo system.

Jack was just starting to relax. He didn't want to ruin the day dwelling on his troubles with the BHR. He wanted to fish and drink, not necessarily in that order. "Same old shit, nothing to worry about. Can we get back to our lines? I think I had a bite before you scared my record-breaking walleye away." Jack smiled, hoping his attempt at humor would shake his uncle from his question.

"Jack, tell me what's going on." UW's tone told Jack his ploy hadn't worked, and the retired military man wouldn't let it go.

Relenting, Jack launched into a tirade. "The government has me by the short hairs. They've injected two Bureau of Harm Reduction Observers into the shop. I tried to resist, but they leaned on Straus Precision, who then threatened to cancel their contract. They've been poking around for a few weeks now. I can't stand it. Every time I turn around, a gray suit is standing there. All they've managed to do is disrupt the place." Jack took a long pull from his beer, then continued. "One of the little pricks had the balls to suggest *manufacturing improvements*. Can you believe that shit? He stood in a shop full of veteran machinists and basically told them they suck at their jobs."

His uncle's gaze went icy, and he turned the music's volume up. "Have you talked to your lawyers?"

Jack's anger bubbled up, and he answered the question with more force than he intended. "Yep. Nothing they can do. Actually, John Hightower, the managing partner at the firm, sounded scared to death that I even called him. His advice was to be as accommodating as possible. Let it blow over."

UW let his gaze linger on Jack for a long minute before speaking. "That's the only way to handle it. They hold the cards, all the cards."

Jack remembered UW owed him an explanation of his own. Eager to change the subject, he asked his uncle about his secretive behavior. His uncle's answer turned his blood to ice.

"Jack, did you notice the utility van parked in front of my house?"

He hadn't and shook his head.

"It arrived at the crack of dawn. No one exited, no one sat in the driver's seat, and none of my neighbors came out to greet them. The name on the truck was *85 Plumbing*. I checked but couldn't find a listing for them. I'm not sure what's happening, but I have my suspicions. For now, just play the game. I'll let you know when it's time to stop playing nice."

UW tuned the radio to an AM talk station and asked Jack to take a seat. He leaned closer to Jack, radiating intensity. "As we speak, the Pentagon is conducting background investigations into every single member of the United States military. Anyone connected in any way to the previous administration will be deemed a security risk and discharged from military service."

UW paused, appearing to struggle with how much he wanted to tell Jack. "That encompasses every aspect of the past admin. If a soldier so much as supported a policy set forth, they are a risk in the eyes of the current administration."

"That sounds unconstitutional. How can they justify that?" Jack interrupted.

"Once they identify a person or a group as a threat, or a clear and present danger, the gloves come off. The Constitution becomes a worthless piece of paper. Individual rights vanish. No one fights back because it's all in the name of safety. That van outside my house tells me I have been deemed a dissenter. I'm a clear and present danger, and they're building a case against me. If they don't find something, they'll make it up."

UW leaned back in his seat and took a hard pull from his beer. "My advice to you stands. Play the game for now. And one last thing. Let your Concealed Carry License expire."

UW was interrupted by a breaking news story blaring over the radio. Washington DC had been locked down. He glanced at Jack and nodded toward the speakers. "Clear and present danger."

CHAPTER 12

STINGER MACHINERY

Jack sat staring at the Form 85OI-Observer Integration. The billable hours listed were astronomical. He would be forced to lay off staff if the BHR's Observers remained imbedded in his business much longer.

The cocky grin on the gray suit awaiting his signature wasn't helping his mood. "How in the actual hell can you justify this?" Jack asked.

The gray suit's smile faltered, but he quickly recovered. "The additional fee is for our consulting services. Please, sign the form. I have lunch plans."

Jack glared at the youngster. "It's ten-thirty; you have plenty of time to make your lunch plans. Now, explain the consulting fees. Because all you've done for the past month is disrupt my business. A business that just a few short months ago was profitable."

"Oh, Mister Stinger, your resistance to change is typical of people your age and political affiliation. You're rooted in the past while the future buzzes around your window, begging to be let in. Fortunately, the BHR has opened that window and ushered in a new, improved way of thinking. One that values worker input over production output."

The gray suit's smug attitude nearly sent Jack into a rage. *Play the game*, his uncle's words replayed in his mind. Regaining control of his emotions, Jack said, "I asked you for an explanation of the consulting fees. I'll add to that the question as to why my political leanings are relevant."

"Sign the Form 85OI, Mister Stinger. Or I'll be forced to update my latest progress report. Negative reports carry harsh consequences. You wouldn't want additional Observers assigned to Stinger Machinery, would you?"

Jack slid the form across the table. "Explain the fees."

The gray suit flushed with anger as he snatched the Form 85OI off Jack's desk and stood to leave. He paused at the door, and without turning around, said, "Tell me, Jack. How is your wife's new position working out?" Then threw up his hand and said, "Don't bother, I already know."

As the gray suit sauntered from his office, Jack fought the urge to bum rush and pummel him. Standing at his desk, Jack yelled at the gray suit's back, "Are you trying to intimidate me by threatening my wife?"

The young man didn't respond as he quickened his pace toward the shop area. Jack followed, rapidly closing the gap between them. "I asked you a question!" Jack shouted.

The gray suit stopped, turned slowly, and said, "Another assumption from an outdated way of thinking. I'll be sure to add it to my progress report. And to answer your question…" a sickly wet smile broke on his face. "My question was not a threat."

"I'll sign the damn form," Jack said, grimacing. "Just leave Lisa out of this. She's not involved with my business."

"Too late, Mister Stinger. The Form 85OI will be submitted as is. You should expect a call from Agent Woods."

CHAPTER 13

JACK AND LISA'S HOME

When he pulled into the driveway, Jack found Lisa sitting on their front porch, the house behind her dark. Something was wrong. He took the Form 85NOF-Notice of Fine, stuffed it into the inside pocket of his Carhartt jacket, and quickly exited his Yukon.

As he hurried up the walkway to the house, he noticed her red-rimmed eyes. "What's wrong?" he asked, worry taking control.

"They did it, Jack."

"Who? And what did they do to you? Are you okay?"

Jack's pace quickened after each question until he was seated next to his wife. Her distant stare pushed him past worry to fear.

"Lisa, what's going on. Did someone hurt you?"

"I worked so hard, Jack. I earned that position, and now it's gone."

Jack's vision went red, his thoughts going back to the gray suit's veiled threat.

"They demoted me, Jack. I'm now a research clerk. An entry-level position, after fifteen years, and all those years working on my degree—they demoted me from R&D Director to research clerk. I'm a chemist, Jack. Not a research clerk! They wouldn't tell me why; they just did it. Came into my office, ordered me to pack my things and move to a cubical in the basement. I'm the only person in the basement!"

Lisa broke into tears, and Jack took her into his arms as she sobbed. He realized what had happened. Her performance wasn't responsible for the demotion. He was, because he hadn't played the game by their rules. But he'd thought it would stop at the fine, never imagining they would attack his family.

After Lisa calmed down, Jack helped her into the house and poured two stiff drinks. He hadn't told her about the incident with the gray suit or the fifty-thousand-dollar fine levied against Stinger Machinery by the Bureau of Harm Reduction.

"Did they give you any indication this was coming, anything at all?"

Lisa set her drink on the coffee table and hugged her knees to her chest on the couch. "Nothing!" she barked. "Not a single solitary thing. The department's projects are all on schedule. Our productivity has improved. Everything was running smoothly."

"Lisa, have you noticed any new employees or unfamiliar faces around the office? Probably over the last two months?"

Confused by Jack's question, Lisa snipped, "What the hell does that have to do with anything, Jack? My career ended today. Who cares if they hired someone new?"

"Lisa, I understand you're upset, but it's important."

She paused, trying to focus on her husband's odd question. Her eyes went wide as she answered, "Yes, a lady started in Corporate Compliance three weeks ago. We called her the gray lady, because she always wore gray suits. It was a newly created position. Everyone figured she was hired because she had connections to someone in upper management. Why?"

Jack pinched the bridge of his nose, fighting back his anger. "I did this. I'm the reason you've been demoted. The Bureau of Harm Reduction started turning the screws on me. It boiled over last week. I refused to sign one of their Form 85s. The BHR Observer made a comment about your new position." Jack looked up to find Lisa's eyes boring into his. "I'm sorry, babe, I'm so sorry. I thought it was just a threat to keep me in line."

Lisa stared at Jack as he watched the woman he treasured transform back into the fighter he'd fallen in love with. "Well, they can kiss my ass! I won't stand for it. I'm submitting my resignation tomorrow. No explanation or long-winded proclamations of how I was treated unfairly. Just my resignation."

Jack smiled, then asked her to get her laptop. "Have they cut off your access to your research? Or the properties you've created?"

Lisa's evil grin told him she knew exactly what they were about to do.

With Lisa sound asleep, Jack eased himself from their bed and snuck downstairs. He picked up the flash drive and gripped it tightly in his hand. He was done playing nice with the government. The midterms were a year away; the American people would punish this administration for its overreach, he was sure of it. It was time to organize to ensure they turned out in overwhelming numbers.

Stinger Machinery wasn't the only business being bullied into submission. He could hear it in his vendors' voices when he talked to them. Pressure was being applied to everyone, and the administration's versions of Nazi Brownshirts were the hammers applying it.

He unplugged his phone from its charger and thumbed through his contacts, pressing send when he found the number he was looking for. "UW, I need to talk. Are you free tomorrow?"

"Well, seeing tomorrow's Thanksgiving, and I'm going to be at your house, I'm sure I have the time."

Jack couldn't believe it; he'd forgotten about Thanksgiving. In a panic, he rushed to the refrigerator and swung open the door, relieved to find their turkey thawing on the bottom self.

"Jack, don't say another word. We'll finish this tomorrow. Get back to bed."

CHAPTER 14

STINGER MACHINERY

Jack stood in front of his team. Missing were the Christmas decorations and holiday cheer usually found adorning the building this time of year. In their place were the hard stares of a team he no longer recognized as the Stinger Machinery family.

They weren't chatting about their plans for the upcoming Christmas holiday. No talk of the gifts they'd purchased or hoped to receive. They stood with the members of their *silos*, avoiding interaction with other silos, all of them glaring at Jack.

Today would have been the day Jack handed out Christmas bonus checks, a tradition dating back to Stinger Machinery's founding. A tradition he would end today. "I'm sorry to inform you that the company can't afford our annual Christmas bonus."

Groans of discontent and gasps of surprise greeted Jack's announcement. The only person not shocked into reaction was his accountant. She broke the news to Jack last week that Stinger's finances were deep in the red. Jack tried to secure the funding to keep the tradition alive and inject much-needed cash into the business, but he quickly learned Stinger Machinery had maxed out its credit lines.

Armin and Randy turned to the group and attempted to calm them down. The room quieted long enough for the lone BHR Observer attending the meeting to toss a bucket of gasoline onto the smoldering embers. "Tell us, Jack. What will your holiday look like? With your executive-level salary and the perks that accompany being a business owner. I'm sure it'll be a lavish event filled with opulent gifts and a gourmet feast. Maybe you'll see fit to bring your table scraps and hand them out to the peasants supporting your lifestyle."

His accountant, Alison, matched Jack's anger at the Observer's statement. The slightly built bean counter hard-stepped in the gray suit's direction and yelled, "You rotten son of a bitch. I see firsthand what's happening to this company, and to Jack. He'll be lucky to avoid bankruptcy." She stood nose to nose with the smug government thug, the Observer daring Alison to act on her fury.

"Alison, I appreciate what you're doing. But now's not the time." Jack turned his attention to the gray suit. "And you. If you'd like to know what my *Christmas* will be like, you're welcome to ask Agent Woods. I'm confident she understands my finances."

The truth was Jack hadn't taken a paycheck from Stinger for two months. Paying for the BHR Observers was draining the company. Jack had saved the Straus contract when he bent a knee to the government. But their orders fell by fifty percent. Orders from his other customers had dropped more significantly, with some disappearing altogether.

Alison had told him that Stinger needed to cut its workforce by twenty percent if they wanted to survive into next year. That conversation took place before Stinger Machinery paid the crippling fine to the Bureau of Harm Reduction.

The BHR Observer huffed his dismissal as he stepped away from Alison. "This is proof that you should unionize. The workers of Stinger Machinery could have written their holiday bonus into their labor contract and forced *Mister* Stinger to share his good fortune." He paused, meeting each stare from Jack's team. "Although your pay would undoubtedly increase, rendering the paltry holiday bonus moot. Such is the strength of collective bargaining."

The self-righteous smile hadn't left the Observer's face as Randy turned to Jack and signed, "Say the word."

Armin had been translating the Observer's speech for Randy and quickly added his support to Randy's offer. Jack smiled. He'd love nothing more than to see the troublemaker laid out on the office floor. But he shook his head, saving the young man a trip to the hospital and his friends from handcuffs.

Jack still believed in his plan to organize other business owners and speak his displeasure through his vote. The BHR had planted the seed and nurtured it every day. He was confident the administration would pay for their actions.

The support of his longtime employees was reassuring but appeared limited to the three defending him. The others were focused on the gray suit. The damage he'd inflicted over the course of his time embedded into Stinger Machinery was irreparable. If the company survived, he'd be forced to rebuild his entire team.

CHAPTER 15

PUBLIC ROOM, SAMMY'S DELI

Randy and Armin asked Jack to join them for a beer, but he declined the offer, intent on greeting any of the twenty-four people he'd invited to Sammy's for their initial meeting.

That was twenty minutes ago and forty minutes past the meeting's scheduled start time. He called some of the listed attendees only to be transferred directly to their voicemail. "Well, time to pack it in." His voice bounced off the empty community room's walls, reminding him of his failure.

A short time ago, Jack would have donated the sandwich trays and tubs of side dishes to the local food bank. But now it was coming home with him. He could no longer afford to be charitable.

He stood to his full six feet to stretch the stress from his back when he caught movement at the entrance. Excited that someone had joined him, he turned to greet the latecomer. His heart sank when he found the self-satisfied grin of Agent Woods leaning against the door frame.

"Huh, appears your attempt at political activism has failed miserably, Jack."

Her appearance explained everything.

"Are we on a first-name basis, Agent Woods?"

"We are not, *Mister* Stinger. You will refer to me as Agent Woods, and I will refer to you however I'd like. You've been *misbehaving*, acting like a petulant child, and I will treat you accordingly."

Her abrasive demeanor caught Jack off guard. She was never friendly, but she'd upped her game today.

"Tell me, Agent Woods. How much does it cost me to fly you to Cleveland? Or is that a burden the American taxpayer shoulders?"

Eyes narrowed, Woods said, "My work is important and demands that I conduct in-person field inspections to ensure no harm comes to our fellow Americans or the Bureau of Harm Reduction Observers. The cost is inconsequential when weighed against safety." She walked to a table and sat, motioning to Jack to do the same.

Taking a seat across from her, Jack rested his chin on laced fingers. "Organizing a group of like-minded individuals is now a security risk?" he asked.

"When it's the same group of people responsible for the situation at our Capitol, it becomes a security concern."

Clear and present danger. His uncle's words rang in his ears.

"However," she said, "the reason for today's visit centers on Stinger Machinery's fine for refusing to sign the Form 85OI. It was brought to my attention that your Form 85PF-Payment of Fine and accompanying check were processed twenty-four hours late. The fine for late payments is two hundred percent of the original fine plus interest accruing at fifty percent of the original fine, daily."

Jack was no accountant, but the math was pretty simple. It was a death sentence. With UW's voice now screaming *play the game*, he responded, "You know I can't afford to pay that ridiculous amount of money. You also know that I mailed my payment in ample time to meet the deadline. So, what's your angle, Agent Woods?"

Woods loved this part. Another broken capitalist searching the maze for that sliver of cheese. The lifeline she'd buried in a labyrinth of paperwork and government bureaucracy. "You obviously haven't been reading the updates we've emailed. The postmark no longer matters. Payments of fines and taxes must arrive three weeks before the predetermined date, or they're considered late. But, in your case, I believe you left the privacy statement acknowledgment checkbox on your Form 85PF blank. This forced our receivables clerk to seek managerial guidance. Unfortunately, her manager was on a two-week vacation. Hence, your payment was late."

Jack's first instinct was to fight, to drag them into court, making a public spectacle of the bureaucratic abuse. Then, recalling his attorney's earlier reaction, he understood he had no way out.

"I can see by your downtrodden expression that you have no way to pay. I've also studied your financial position, both personal and business, so I know it to be a fact." A slimy grin broke on her face. "But, never fear. Your government is here to help."

"Help, you say? Help me out of the problems created by the government? Is that your intent? To fix the issues your bureaucracy produced? So, enlighten me, Agent Woods. What form will my government *assistance* take?"

Brushing off his commentary, Agent Woods reached into her briefcase, retrieving a stack of papers. "The government is prepared to loan you the funds required to support your business. Of course, we will hold Stinger Machinery as collateral."

Jack's vision tilted hard right as panic took root. That was her play the entire time: control of Stinger Machinery. "No, thank you. I'll find the funding on my own."

Her smile disappeared, replaced by pursed lips. Suddenly her eyebrows arched while she slowly shook her head. "This offer expires the second you leave this room."

CHAPTER 16

ONE YEAR POST INAUGURATION, PRESIDENTIAL EMERGENCY OPERATIONS CENTER

Robert's daily PEOC visits had grown unbearable. Eden's psychological condition, already difficult to manage, had begun deteriorating rapidly. Roberts worried they would lose him long before the time was right.

He set his gaze on Eden as he paced the briefing room, mumbling about not seeing daylight in a month, being the President, and getting back to the Oval Office. Truth be told, Roberts was running the country while the President and Vice President sat safely locked away in the Presidential Emergency Operations Center with their families.

For her part, Vice President Genus seemed to enjoy her time underground. She held no meetings, made no decisions, and avoided staff interactions at all costs. She spent most of her days in sweatpants watching movies piped into the PEOC via closed circuit and eating extraordinary amounts of junk food.

Roberts controlled the information they received, newsfeeds were edited prior to being viewed, and members of Congress were forbidden to meet with either of them. Restricting congressional access proved easier than expected. A well-timed *intelligence leak* stating that domestic terrorists had conspired with members of Congress was all it took. The Secret Service acted on the intelligence immediately by tightening access to Eden. Now, only his top aides had clearance to enter the PEOC. And Roberts controlled those aides, meaning none of them found their way to either Eden or Genus.

Roberts had them right where he wanted them, isolated and blind. But his media allies were growing restless. The video clip of the Edens and Genuses enjoying Thanksgiving dinner hadn't silenced the voices screaming to hear from the leader of the free world. He couldn't stall any longer. It was time to risk putting the feeble idiot in front of a camera.

Telling Eden that very thing had created the current situation. He'd been shuffling around, mumbling incoherently for the last half hour. Eden insisted he leave the PEOC and address America from the National Plaza. Something Roberts couldn't allow. The man could barely dress himself, let alone speak to the public in an uncontrolled environment. *He's liable to declare war on South Korea.* The thought forced a chuckle.

Eden slammed to a stop and pivoted to face Roberts. "Do I amuse you, Mister Roberts?"

Thankfully, Roberts was holding his phone and held it up for Eden to see. "No sir, Mister President. A story about children eating laundry detergent popped up on my feed. Where are their parents?"

"Tell me, Roberts. How is it your phone gets a signal, but the President of the United States' phone can't?"

Surprised by Eden's sudden lucidity, Roberts at first stumbled through his response but quickly recovered. "The ability for the terrorists to locate you by tracking your signal is unknown and poses a threat. If they can pinpoint your location, they may launch an attack. We're unsure if they possess the resources to hit this location with high explosives or other heavy weapons capable of reaching the PEOC."

"Sounds like typical DC hogwash. They, whoever *they* are, couldn't possibly have that amount of destructive power without our government knowing about it. And another thing, how is it possible the entire intelligence community has been unsuccessful in locating these domestic terrorists? It's been a month, an entire damn month, and they've found not one of them? They have no leads, executed no arrests, and don't have so much as the name of a single member of their organization? Bullshit, Roberts, it's impossible!"

Eden's sharp dress-down put Roberts on his heels for the first time since joining the administration during the run-up to the election. As campaign manager, he'd had lively debates with Eden, but nothing approaching this level of aggression.

"Mister President, all the intelligence we've gathered suggests a well-organized, heavily armed group numbering in the thousands. They possess the technology required to cover their tracks. We believe them to be using alternative social media platforms, which don't track or harvest user data, for recruiting new members. Something we're aiming to end. Cut them off at the knees, so to speak."

"Come on, man," Eden interrupted. "You use a lot of words to say very little. Something I'm growing tired of. Now, arrange a damn public address on the National Plaza."

Roberts' phone buzzed, bringing Eden's tirade to an end. Before he could answer, Eden's moment of clarity vanished, and his eyes clouded over as he struggled to find a seat.

Roberts glanced at his phone, and panic gripped him. Rosos was calling. He quickly excused himself from the room, an action Eden either didn't notice or simply hadn't been coherent enough to acknowledge.

Rushing to one of the private conversation booths lining the walls of the briefing room, Roberts slammed the door and answered. "Mister Rosos, with all due respect, this is a most inopportune time for your call. Can it wait?"

He listened to his keeper for a long moment, then replied, "Sir, although your plan would undoubtedly be successful, it seems rather harsh."

Again, Roberts was silent. Rosos' words sent a chill down his spine. "Oh, I didn't realize you were monitoring my conversation with Eden. I agree, the man is being difficult, but I hardly believe it rises to a level requiring the actions you're proposing."

Rosos' sharp response told Roberts he had crossed a line. "Yes sir, I'll invite the Speaker of the House to meet with Eden immediately. But sir, I'm requesting that the second half of your plan spare one person. My aunt is the Governor of California. Can you find it in your heart to forgo including California?"

Roberts screwed his eyes shut. Rosos' intention to accelerate his plan was absolute. "So be it. And to answer your question, yes sir, I'm confident your plan will have the desired effect on the American commonality. Good day, sir."

Roberts exited the private booth. Thick fog seemed to settle around him. His unsteady legs carried him to the highly polished conference table. As he supported his faltering body against it, he locked Eden in a withering stare and said, "You couldn't hold it together for another year? You're a useless waste of flesh."

Eden's empty eyes continued tracking some distant memory. Roberts' comment should have sparked a skin-melting fire in the talking head. Instead, the shell of a man simply mumbled and flashed his best politician's smile.

The realization that Rosos was always listening to him and may have heard every word Roberts spoke for over a year sent a chill down his spine. Was he next on Rosos' list?

In disgust, Roberts turned his back to the President and quickly found Speaker Rye's number and pressed send. "Madam Speaker, the President has requested your presence in the PEOC, immediately."

"Please refer to me as Speaker Rye; it is more inclusive. I shouldn't have to remind you of the need to erase gendered language from your vocabulary. What does he want? I'm not comfortable leaving my secured office. Unless this is an emergency, I prefer to video chat with him."

Roberts remembered why he despised Rye as soon as she spoke. Perhaps Rosos' plan would yield some benefit to him after all. "Of course, Speaker Rye, I apologize. The stress of the current situation has me a bit out of sorts and reverting to some bad habits. I'm afraid it is an emergency. I'll dispatch the armored executive branch SUV. It will deliver you to the heavily guarded entrance on H Street. Our intelligence indicates that the terrorists are unaware it exists. You mustn't share with anyone that you're meeting with Eden, not even your most trusted aides."

Roberts waited as Rye cleared her gin-soaked voice. "How very cloak and dagger of you to use the H Street entrance. But, I suppose the times we live in are guiding your actions. I'll expect a full security force to be waiting at the entrance."

Relief and dread battled for Roberts' attention as he spoke. "Very good. I'll dispatch the SUV and security detail now. Be ready in fifteen minutes. I'll see you soon."

Roberts disconnected the call and, with his back to Eden, told him to prepare for an emergency meeting with Rye, to which he received no response. Picking up the closed-circuit phone, he dialed Genus' private quarters. "Vice President Genus. The President is calling an emergency meeting. House Speaker Rye is en route. The President has requested your presence."

Several seconds of huffing and puffing passed before she responded, "Oh, whatever. I'll be down momentarily. This better be important and not just more of his crazy ramblings."

"I can assure you, Vice President, this is very important."

***

Roberts received notice that Rye was approaching the drop-off point and activated the closed-circuit cameras covering the entrance on H Street. Tapping a command into the video display brought up the feed from H Street.

The image it broadcast caused Roberts' stomach to clench. He knew that Rosos planned to move against the Second Amendment, but he'd never imagined this would be his catalyst. He blamed Eden for what was about to happen. If he hadn't been so damned difficult or incompetent, this could have been avoided.

The three of them watched as the SUV slowed to a stop and activated its hazards. A team of six Secret Service members, three on either side of the armored SUV's passenger door, moved into position.

Roberts wanted to close his eyes but couldn't. He felt the same urge as when passing a terrible car accident: He had to watch. After several seconds, Rye emerged from the enormous vehicle and said something unintelligible to the Secret Service agent closest to her.

Something happened out of camera range, causing two agents to reach for Rye while a third spun in the commotion's direction and dropped to a knee, leaving Rye exposed.

An instant after the agent knelt, Rye's head snapped back violently, and her body slumped from the grasp of the now blood-covered agents attempting to protect her. The chaotic scene ended when the agents moved to shield Rye's body and rushed her back into the SUV, which quickly sped away. Roberts made a mental note of the actions taken by the Secret Service agent who'd gone to a knee. *Good to know. I thought the SS was impenetrable.*

Genus' gasp pulled him back to his surroundings. Her hand covered her mouth, but her expression was clear; the assassination of Speaker Ann Rye had elicited its desired effect. The woman was terrified. Any doubt the threat was real vanished the instant the sniper's round slammed through Rye's skull.

Swallowing the bile rising in his throat, Roberts glanced from the VP to Eden. The President met his stare and, in a childlike voice, asked, "What happened to Ann? She looks hurt."

"She's dead, you idiot," Genus screamed. "She's dead, and we're next." Eyes blazing with fear, she locked onto Roberts. "Get me out of here. They're just waiting for us to show ourselves. If they can kill Rye despite all the security, it's only a matter of time until they kill me."

As Genus stormed from the conference center, Eden, with a bemused look, said, "Wow, she seems really upset." Pausing for a moment, and seemingly unaffected by Rye's death, he said, "I guess this means I won't be speaking from the National Mall anytime soon?"

CHAPTER 17

MOUNT WEATHER EMERGENCY OPERATIONS CENTER

Roberts fidgeted as the phone rang, his anxiety growing. *Please answer.* His plea was answered when his aunt's voice filled the speaker. "Well hello, Thad. I'm sorry, Chief of Staff Roberts. How is my favorite nephew?"

Roberts closed his eyes, willing himself to remain calm. "Aunt Edna. Or should I call you Governor Roberts?" Their wordplay had started shortly after his appointment to Eden's administration.

He soaked in the sweet sound of her laugh, promising himself he'd never forget it.

"To what do I owe the honor of your call, Thad? I imagine, with current events, you've got your hands full. Tell me, have you made any progress locating the terrorists?"

Roberts glanced at his watch. Two minutes till noon, Pacific. "Aunt Edna," he said, a slight tremor in his voice. "Let's not waste time on my troubles. How have you been? Are you in the Capitol building?"

His aunt, noticing the stress in her nephew's voice, said, "You sound out of sorts, Thad. Are you feeling ill? You mustn't allow your position to affect your health. You should visit me;

we'll take a weekend in Sonoma. Nothing melts the worries away like a bottle of Syrah."

"Oh, that sounds lovely. Tell me, are you in the Capitol?" he asked again, building a mental image of her surroundings.

"Thad." Her voice was stern and crystal clear. "What's wrong? You're worrying me."

"Please, Aunt Edna, just tell me where you are. I'm... I'm imagining the sun warming your face on a beautiful California afternoon."

Worry creased her features as she rose from her desk, taking a position at her office window overlooking the lush grounds. "I'm working from the mansion. My security detail insisted I do so until the terrorists have been dealt with. I'm in my office window; it is a beautiful day indeed. Thad, please tell me what's wrong. Can I help?"

His watch now read one minute till noon. He shut his eyes tight, forcing a tear to trace the curve of his cheek. "Oh, it sounds beautiful. Just like you." His words were choked with emotion.

"Thad, tell me what's happening. And tell me this instant."

The blurred hands of his Rolex showed thirty seconds to noon. "Aunt Edna, you've always been my favorite. I love you with all of my heart. You know that, right? It's important that you know that. You cared for me more than my parents. I owe you so very much. Tell me you know how I feel about you." His proclamations came in rapid-fire succession.

The sound of shattering glass ripped through his mind as his head sagged to the table's icy surface. "I'm so sorry."

***

He watched through his scope as the suppressed .338 Lapua round snapped his target's head back. He smiled. Nine hundred and eight meters, just over half a mile, stood as his second-longest kill shot. The operation was in jeopardy until she moved to the window, presenting a perfectly framed target to his crosshairs.

"Target neutralized," he reported to his keepers as he wiped sweat from his forehead, the jagged scar running its width standing out in stark relief.

The same message relayed six more times, from across the country, on that beautifully sunny day.

CHAPTER 18

MOUNT WEATHER EMERGENCY OPERATIONS CENTER

Roberts placed the prepared remarks on the conference table in front of Eden and made ready for the inevitable. The President's medication regimen had yielded minor improvements in his cognitive ability. Eden bounced into lucid states more often and remained cognizant longer than Roberts remembered during his entire tenure in the administration.

It should have been a welcome development, but he quickly learned a coherent Eden was harder to manage than the mentally vacant one. Eden had pushed back on every proposal for addressing the public presented to him. He continued to insist on delivering his remarks from the National Mall, as a show of strength.

Roberts couldn't allow that to happen. Putting Eden in the open meant the media would insist on attending. A live feed from the media would make it impossible for him to cut the feed if Eden suddenly went blank. It would happen from this room on Roberts' terms.

"Mister President, this is the speech you will give, and you will deliver it from this location. Have I been clear?"

Eden's hard glare told Roberts that he had indeed been clear, and Eden wasn't pleased. "I'm sorry, son. I'm the Commander-in-Chief; *you* are a lackey. You're employed as a political favor to a donor. Something you appear to have forgotten."

Eden stared at Roberts until he picked up the speech. He flipped through the pages in dramatic fashion, giving a cursory review to each. Roberts understood what was happening. Eden was looking for the speech's "punch." They would not waste this crisis. It was the rule of every political hack in government. He was searching for the words the American public would find most egregious, the freedom the government would crush as a result of the domestic terrorists' actions. He quickly found them.

"Are you joking? You want me to tell the American people that we're *suspending*"—Eden air quoted—"the Second Amendment? Tell me, Roberts. How does one *suspend* a portion of the Bill of Rights? We'll have a thousand lawsuits filed against us thirty seconds after I finish my speech. Not to mention we weren't going to tackle gun control until after the midterms. I can name half a dozen Blue Dogs that will literally shit themselves if I even mention gun control before November."

Roberts interrupted Eden's rant by slamming his hand on the conference room table. "The politics of yesterday will sink this administration. We're moving on this now. It's vital that we use this opportunity to cripple the Two-A. Seven Governors in these United States were assassinated two weeks ago. Including my aunt. It's time to act, to end this terrorist insurgence NOW!"

That Eden didn't recognize the beauty of the strategy was infuriating. His ignorance of the sacrifices Roberts had made for this to happen nearly blinded him with rage.

The bureaucrats glared across the table at one another, entrenched in their positions. The staring contest resembled one between playground rivals until Roberts glanced at the monitor displaying the feed from Raven Rock Mountain, military complex.

They had secured Vice President Genus at the military complex under the guise of preserving the executive branch of government in case a breach occurred at one of the secured sites. In reality, Roberts simply couldn't stand being near her.

She'd been silently watching the tense exchange and startled when Roberts addressed her. "Vice President Genus, are you alone?"

Her eyes wide, she nodded her confirmation.

"I mean you no insult," Roberts began. "But I'll need you to show me. Please move the camera around the room. What I'm about to say is top secret."

Roberts watched Genus fumble to remove the video camera from its mount and pan around the room. She was indeed alone.

"Mister President, I'm going to play a video. I'm certain you'll change your position after you watch it."

Roberts punched a command into the keyboard, controlling the monitors hanging on the walls in the secured room where he and Eden sat. Grinning, he leaned his chair back as the video fluttered to life.

***

As the video ended, Roberts glanced in the President's direction. Eden's flushed complexion told Roberts he had him by the balls. "Mister President. I'm confident you grasp the ramifications if this video were to fall into the wrong hands. Or get *leaked* by a rogue staffer. I mean, you're on video telling the CEOs of the world's largest social media companies to suppress free speech. Thanking them for colluding with your campaign to win the election. My perspective is that if you're not troubled by crushing the First Amendment, crushing the Second Amendment should be even less concerning. Prepare for your address to the nation, sir."

CHAPTER 19

JACK AND LISA'S HOME

Jack gazed at his wife as they sat on their family room couch. She was trying to enjoy the Godzilla movie marathon he'd insisted on watching. In reality, she was just trying to stay awake through the classic Sci-Fi movies. It was the first opportunity they'd found in weeks to relax and not worry about work or preparing for a job interview. And they'd decided to spend a quiet evening at home. Jack sprang the Godzilla marathon on her after they settled in. If she'd known his plan, she would have thrown a fit and dragged him to dinner at some expensive restaurant where he couldn't pronounce anything on the menu.

Lisa's job search was rougher than expected. She'd been on half a dozen, and each followed a similar pattern. She always made it through the initial interview with strong positive reactions from the interviewer and performed equally strong during her second interview. Then the bottom would drop out. She wouldn't hear from the company. When she followed up, she'd be told that after contacting references or past employers, they'd awarded a rival candidate the position.

She suspected that BYT-Chemical was behind the string of rejections, but she couldn't prove it. She'd reached out to several friends at BYT, but they acted as if she had the plague. One actually asked that she never contact him again.

Jack recognized what was happening. They had blackballed Lisa. No doubt the Bureau of Harm Reduction was behind it. They'd recently applied more pressure at Stinger Machinery, as if the financially crippling loan wasn't enough. They'd continued encouraging the machinists and office staff to unionize. Something Jack had never discouraged but couldn't afford. He paid his employees, all of them, well above industry standard coupled with the best health insurance Stinger Machinery could afford. Yet, somehow, the BHR Observers determined Stinger's compensation package was lacking. After the Christmas bonus debacle, they redoubled their efforts to convince his team they were underpaid and underappreciated. And it was working.

He'd also noticed a disturbing trend. The Bureau of Harm Reduction Observers were dividing his team by race, ethnicity, gender, or any label they could assign. What was once a family environment quickly devolved into a workplace full of smoldering resentment. He wondered how long it could go on before it imploded. *Divide and concur*, he mused.

Pushing the negative thoughts away, he smiled at his wife as her head bobbed, losing her fight to stay awake. "Lisa," he said in his best singsong voice, "it's time for bed."

Her eyes snapped open, and she struggled to identify her surroundings. "What? The movie isn't over," she stammered. "I'm beginning to understand why you enjoy these…. Oh Jack, I can't. These movies are awful. Can we please watch something else?"

Jack laughed through his response. "No, but you can go to bed. You can't keep your eyes open, and it has nothing to do with

Godzilla. The greatest movies ever made, I might add. So scoot. I'll be up soon."

He leaned over and kissed his wife and shooed her from the couch.

"Okay, okay, I'm going. Enjoy your stupid movie!"

"Aw, is Lisa a grumpy bear because she's sleepy?" Jack was pushing his luck, and he knew it. Lisa was always cranky when she woke up, and he always poked the hornet's nest.

"JACK, why do you insist on risking your life when I wake up?" Lisa snipped as she trundled to the stairs and off to bed. "Don't stay up too late. Remember we're going to the Rock Hall tomorrow, and I want to get there early," she added over her shoulder.

"Yes, dear. I'll be up after Godzilla kicks Megalon's ass."

Lisa had just cleared the room when Jack's phone buzzed. Annoyed with what he assumed to be another telemarketer selling him an extended car warranty, he prepared an epic salutation for the unfortunate caller.

Surprise and worry gripped him when he saw his uncle's number displayed on his phone's screen. "What's wrong?" he said as he bolted upright on the couch.

"You watching Eden's press conference?"

"Press conference? It's a little late at night for a press conference. Shouldn't he have called a lid at noon?" Jack paused, the gravity of the situation sinking in. "I thought he was in hiding?"

Jack could hear UW's television blaring in the background, something he'd been meaning to ask him about. He suspected his uncle was losing his hearing.

"Turn it on, now. Call me when it's over." UW hung up, leaving Jack with a sinking feeling.

He found the remote and changed the channel. It wasn't hard to find the dead-eyed talking head. The presser was being broadcast on every national network.

Jack watched as Eden fumbled through a stack of papers laid out before him. He certainly wasn't in the Oval Office. Jack had never seen a sitting president give an address from the location Eden was in.

The camera zoomed in tight on Eden. He appeared lost as he continued searching the papers for something unknown to the television audience. Jack noticed his lips moving as if he was talking to himself. His hand suddenly went to his ear, and he jerked his head to face the camera a split second later.

With his lizard-like smile, he launched into his speech: "My fellow Americans."

"Not a good sign," Jack said to the empty room, commenting on the opening line usually reserved for presidents delivering terrible news.

***

Twenty minutes later, Jack sat bewildered on his couch, trying to process the words spoken by President Eden, but he couldn't wrap his head around them. He rubbed his temples, fighting to contain the headache gaining strength in his forehead.

He stood, intending to retrieve some aspirin from the kitchen when his phone buzzed. UW was calling, and Jack was confident the man was seething.

"Can you believe that shit?" UW's voice barked through the speaker.

"No, I can't. How can he *suspend* the Second Amendment? It's in the Bill of Rights. He can't do that. And declaring a national emergency is insanity. We have the most powerful intelligence agencies in the world. How is it they haven't found these so-called domestic terrorists?"

"Jack, you missed the key sentence. He declared a public health crisis. He can do anything he sees fit to keep the American people safe. I'll ask you the same question I asked at Thanksgiving and Christmas. Do you think organizing a group of business owners to vote in the midterms will make a difference?"

Jack believed in America's political system. He didn't trust a single politician on either side of the aisle. Professional liars, all of them. *Vote for the liar who lies least* was his motto. But he believed in the system, in the American people using their power to right political wrongs.

"I do, and I think Eden's speech will solidify the group I've been trying to organize. People will see what's happening. They'll realize their rights are being stripped away one at a time. It's the classic *slow drip*: one freedom taken away for whatever reason, another under the illusion of public safety. They'll see it and will act on it. I'm trying again to pull a meeting together. I'd still like you to join us."

The background noise at UW's house seemed to increase in volume before his uncle spoke. "Jack, I agree they'll see it. But they won't do anything about it. Comfort Bias is real. I want you to think about that." UW paused. "Do you still have your dad's hunting rifles?"

The question threw Jack. "Yeah, They're in my gun safe. Clean and inspect them every year. Why?"

"Good. Bring them to my house and any of your guns. Leave the safe-queens behind. Put them in a duffle. That monster duffle bag you have, the one we use for camping, should do the trick. Load them into your Yukon from the garage. Pull into my garage when you get here. I'll see you in an hour."

"What's going on?" Jack blurted.

"Just do it. And do it tonight. You need to understand—this isn't going away until they achieve their objectives, whatever they are. Get moving."

UW ended the call and Jack was left standing in his kitchen, confused and with a growing sense of unease. UW knew more than he was sharing. But he trusted him and his instincts and did as he was told.

As he drove to his uncle's house in an SUV full of guns and ammunition, he flipped on the radio to hear how the pundits were reacting. Every political hack alive had found their way onto one talk show or another. The radio stations had brought in their most popular hosts to cover reaction to Eden's speech. The airwaves were full of hollow proclamations to fight back against government overreach.

He had tried logging into his personal Chirp account before heading out, forgetting his account had been deleted, just like his business account, months ago. But as he listened to the callers, a trend became clear. Chirp and Friend Me had cut everyone off. Social media had gone dark. The action only fed conspiracy theories that the government was plotting against the American people. To what end became the subject of heated debates between callers and hosts.

Jack, disgusted, turned the radio off as Eden supporters elbowed their way into the conversation. And like good little sheep, they supported everything the President proposed, droning on about the evils of guns, citing the assassination of government officials across the country, and claiming the state of emergency and declared health crisis were both needed and welcomed policies which would ensure public safety. "Trading your freedom for safety! Franklin was right. You deserve neither." Jack's voice bounced around the empty SUV, and its volume startled him. He was angrier than he realized.

Jack pulled into UW's garage a few moments later and noted the utility van still parked in front of his uncle's house. "85 Plumbing must have a big job," he said to his uncle as the garage door closed behind him.

UW shushed Jack by placing a finger to his own lips. He hurried to the radio sitting atop his workbench and turned it on and cranked the volume up.

"Move the duffle to the kitchen. I'll get it ready for our camping trip later." UW's eyes were searching Jack's for understanding. When Jack didn't answer, he said, "Did you pack your cold-weather gear? The temperatures are dipping into the thirties next week."

Jack, catching on to what was happening, said, "They're in the duffle. I'm looking forward to it. It's been a while since we've hit the trail together."

UW smiled and nodded as a look of relief spread across his features. "Time for a cup of coffee with your old uncle?"

Jack checked his watch. He didn't have the time. It was late, and he had to get up early, per Lisa's orders. But Jack knew his uncle. UW wasn't asking; he was telling Jack to make time. "Sure,

I can squeeze a cup in. But you'll have to turn your radios down. I can hardly hear myself think!"

His uncle shook his head, again motioning for Jack to be quiet as he bobbed his head towards the doorway leading to his house.

Jack followed his uncle into the large kitchen and found an equally loud talk radio program blaring from an under-cabinet-mounted Bose stereo. "UW, I've got to ask: Are you having trouble hearing?"

His uncle chuckled at the question and shook his head while pointing towards the front of the house. He mouthed, "85 Plumbing."

Alarms rang in Jack's head. Could his uncle be suffering a mental break causing paranoid delusions? Jack glanced in the direction UW indicated with his outstretched arm and saw the 85 Plumbing utility van visible through the partially opened blinds covering a large picture window.

Jack let his gaze linger and noticed a flash of light in the cab, as if a door opened then quickly shut. He turned to his uncle, eager to understand what the hell was happening. To avoid being shushed again, he signed, "Do you remember how to sign?"

UW's eyes lit up as he responded, "I do. Take a seat, Jack. We need to talk."

CHAPTER 20

CLEVELAND POLICE UNIT 12

Officer Peter Mathews slammed his squad car to a stop just before exiting the Center Street swing bridge. A protester darted out, tossed a garbage can in his direction, and melted into the mob occupying Heritage Park, just east of the bridge.

"What in the actual hell was that?" Edgar Vasquez barked, his hand on the door handle as he vacillated between chasing their assailant and keeping his ass planted firmly in his seat.

Mathews smiled, the dashboard lights highlighting his scarred face. "They still hate us, Vasquez. Nothing has changed." His young partner struggled with the events of the last month. A rookie, with a year on the force, Vasquez believed in people and struggled under the delusion that they respected police officers. So the past two weeks had been hard on him. Mathews could see the *crust* forming, but he had much to learn.

The endless protests, which always managed to turn into full-blown riots, had been relentless in their pace. Three a day, resulting in hundreds of arrests and dozens of injured officers. It promised to break the department's back. His city was transforming into a war zone.

During his eight years in the Army and twenty-nine years on the force, he'd witnessed nothing like it. The coordination of these groups astonished him. They hit in waves, stretching the department across the city, keeping them in a reactionary posture twenty-four hours a day. Each group supported a different cause, but the recent killings of several government officials gave the anti-gun groups the loudest voice. Mathews' instincts told him that no matter the cause, the planning was centralized. They displayed too many similarities not to be connected: same tactics, identical clothes, and matching piles of bricks and frozen water bottles. The violence spread to neighboring cities, making it impossible for the departments in those cities to dispatch additional officers to assist the beleaguered CPD.

"Take your hand off the door handle. We're staying in the car."

Vasquez turned to meet Mathews' stare. "We're the police; we're supposed to stop this from happening."

"And we will. After our backup arrives. You run at that crowd now, they'll tear you apart. At which point I'll be forced to shoot someone. I'm two days away from retiring, and I'd like to avoid the red tape. We wait and watch. Everyone lives if we do that."

Cutting off Vasquez's reply, Mathews grabbed the radio and called in an update on the situation. The response from Dispatch was unsettling. "Unit Twelve, no additional units are available. Proceed to East Ninth and Chester to assist with crowd control."

Mathews rubbed his face with one meaty paw before responding. "Dispatch, Unit Twelve en route to Ninth and Chester." He tossed the radio to the cruiser's floor and slammed it into reverse.

The sight of the retreating police car garnered cheers of victory from the mob and emboldened them to rush in its direction while hurling bricks and insults at the officers. Mathews used all three of the Ford's mirrors to navigate the narrow passageway. He realized he needed to get them off the bridge before the rioters swarmed their path.

Running for his life wasn't how he'd envisioned his final days on the force. Yet, that's exactly what was happening. His thoughts shattered when a black hoodie appeared in his rearview mirror less than twenty-five yards away. Mathews' foot left the gas pedal as he prepared to slam on the brakes the same instant a brick crashed through the front windshield, missing his head by inches.

Instinct took control, and he stood on the gas pedal, rocketing the cruiser toward the human roadblock standing its path.

Panic building, Vasquez watched in the side mirror as the car halved the distance to the end of the bridge. Yet the anarchist defiantly held his ground. When the hooded man disappeared behind the squad car's girth, Vasquez braced for impact. His mind raced through the potential outcomes, each involving him and his partner dying at the hands of the rioters converging on the bridge from Heritage Park.

"Hold on!" Mathews screamed above the overburdened transmission's whine.

Vasquez's right hand dropped to his sidearm as his left gripped the dashboard. He was tossed against the passenger door the next instant, then slammed to the seatback as Mathews executed a perfect J-turn and accelerated down Center Street.

"Did you hit him?" Vasquez asked.

"No, little bastard lost his nerve at the last second." Mathews glanced over at his partner and said, "But I would have. They had us hemmed in. And that brick removed all doubt about their intentions."

***

Nine hours later, with the icy February morning sun illuminating the smoldering city, Officer Vasquez pulled to a stop in front of Mathews' house. Their ride had been quiet, both men exhausted after twelve hours of battle in Cleveland's streets.

Mathews had dozed during the brief journey from Headquarters to his home on West 11th, in Tremont. His eyes fluttered open at the squeak of Vasquez's jalopy's brakes, and he rolled his head towards his partner. "Having second thoughts?"

Vasquez shook his head. "No, not yet. But Maria is. She asked me to quit the force last week. It's hard on her. Being pregnant isn't helping. She asked me what would happen to her and our baby if I get killed. She wasn't looking for an answer, just wanted me thinking about the future."

"Ouch, that had to sting. What'd you say? And for the love of God, please tell me you didn't prattle on about this being your dream job."

Vasquez's crooked smile told Mathews that's exactly what his partner did.

"Oh, you dumbass! I should beat you on her behalf."

After a much needed laugh, Vasquez asked, "You sure about retiring? You're still young, man. You got a solid ten years left. And the way you work out and eat all that healthy crap you call food, you're in better shape than most newbies."

Mathews had never been more sure about anything. He was done being a cop. Hell, the only reason he'd stayed this last year was to help with Vasquez's training. He liked the kid, wanted him to be successful, so he'd pushed retirement off.

At fifty-five, he figured he'd overstayed his welcome on the force by at least two years. He'd started thinking about retirement after he set the department record for being punched in the face, and he had the scars to prove it.

"Vasquez, you are correct, I'm a fine physical specimen." His statement sent Vasquez into hysterics. "But it's time. I used to know these streets. Hell, I grew up on them. But things are changing, brother. I give you credit for wanting to stay. I just can't. And with the defund talk swirling around, I figure I'm saving someone's job."

The banging of his neighbors' screen door interrupted him. "Son of a bitch."

Vasquez laughed again. "Still loving your new neighbors, I see."

"You haven't seen them in action. Hang around a minute, you'll love the show. And their baby smells like poop. Nasty little thing."

Vasquez broke into uncontrollable laughter. His partner's neighbors had arrived mid-summer, and the stories Mathews told about the couple seemed like fiction, something out of Hollywood. He had to witness it for himself.

"Okay, thirty seconds after I get out of the car, Thatcher, the skinny-jeans guy on the porch. He's going to storm to the property line and lecture me on the wrongs of my profession. With that teaser, I bid you adieu. I'll see you in the morning, same bat-time, same bat-channel."

Mathews exited Vasquez's car and tossed his duty belt over his shoulder before heading up his driveway as his partner monitored his wristwatch's second hand. At the twenty-seven second mark, Thatcher made his move.

With stiff legs wrapped in filthy skinny jeans, and hands curled into fists at his sides, he stormed across his yard. "Excuse me, *Officer* Mathews. We have requested numerous times that you conceal your gun, your device of oppression and murder, when you arrive home. We view the display of your instrument of death as an act of violence."

Mathews glanced to his partner to find him crying with laughter. Turning back to his neighbor, he said, "Hey, Thatcher, how ya been? How's the baby?"

On cue, Margot, spelled Margaux, as she often reminded Mathews when they spoke, pushed through their door. "Thatcher, don't waste your time with thick-headed boot lickers. The city is revolting, showing them how we really feel." Her droopy eyelids were a perfect representation of the pseudo-intellectual snot she was.

"Hey, *Margaux*, good to see you," Mathews offered.

Mathews was convinced the filthy Kurta she wore represented the only piece of clothing she owned. He'd never seen her in anything but the long, tunic-like rag.

"I don't share your sentiment, *Officer* Mathews. Now please acquiesce to my husband's appeal and hide that gawdawful weapon. Must you flaunt your power over the oppressed everywhere you go?"

Mathews took in their yard and the ankle-high grass poking through a light snow cover that hadn't been mowed since they moved in. "Hey, you kids want to come over for dinner tonight?"

Thatcher, who had been fine with his wife taking over the conversation, suddenly found his voice. "Are you insane? We find it intolerable living next door to a murderer. We will never break bread with one!" The skeletal-thin man's face flushed with anger as he pushed his horn-rimmed glasses back into place over his bulging eyes.

"Oh, too bad. I was going to offer you the use of my lawnmower, maybe some other lawn equipment. Help get you ready for spring."

Mathews could hear Vasquez's roaring laughter from the street and forced himself to remain straight-faced.

"Hey, did you look up your name like I suggested? I'm telling you, it means roofer, or roof-thatcher, to be exact. Kinda ironic, seeing your roof needs to be replaced."

Thatcher's wild hair and patchy beard nearly ignited into flame by the time Mathews finished. He stepped towards Mathews, toeing the property line. It seemed he knew the law well enough to understand that the second he left his property, he'd be considered the aggressor if a physical altercation ensued.

Margaux rushed to her husband's side, again injecting herself into the confrontation. "You'd just love for Thatcher to cross the property line so you could execute him like you have so many others. Well, we won't give you the pleasure. Come, Thatcher, it's Angus' feeding time."

Mathews' smile remained plastered on his face. He knew the couple videoed each of their encounters, waiting for the day they pushed him too far and he reacted. Truth be told, he'd love to tie Thatcher into a knot while his wife watched, but he wouldn't give them the satisfaction.

He watched the couple back away toward their porch, keeping an eye, and the lens of Thatcher's iPhone (poking just above the breast pocket of his grungy flannel), focused on him. "So, no dinner?"

CHAPTER 21

DOWNTOWN CLEVELAND, TWENTY-FOUR HOURS LATER

Mathews pulled Vasquez's limp body to safety as a second brick smashed to the pavement where his partner's head had been a split second prior. He screamed for Vasquez to wake up, to get to his feet. They had to run, to escape the mob working its way up East Fourth Street.

The officers had been cut off from the riot detail they'd been assigned to an hour earlier. This group, the one bearing down on them, had materialized from a small parking lot hidden between two of Mathews' favorite restaurants. He and Vasquez had turned north onto Fourth from Prospect Avenue, intending to link up with the primary riot detail on Euclid Avenue when it happened. Within seconds they faced roughly fifty anarchists' hell-bent on burning the city to the ground.

Mathews had yelled at Vasquez to withdraw while he covered their retreat. Armed only with pepper-ball guns and riot shields, they were no match for the brick-throwing, club-wielding "peaceful" protesters who'd just laid eyes on them.

Before he'd even finished his sentence, Vasquez lay sprawled on the ground, bleeding from a gash on his forehead, a bloody brick resting inches away.

Mathews realized his efforts to wake Vasquez were futile. A wave of panic washed over him. Was his friend dead? He rested Vasquez against a burnt-out husk of an abandoned car and radioed the most dreaded of all police communications: *Officer down.*

After making the distress call, Mathews attached Vasquez's riot shield to the man's tactical vest to protect his body from anything the rioters hurled at them. He heaved him into a fireman's carry and broke from the cover of the car. With Vasquez bouncing on his shoulder, he sent three pepper balls into the crowd emerging from East Fourth onto Prospect. He hoped it would at least slow them down enough to allow backup to arrive.

It didn't work, and to his horror, a smaller group suddenly appeared to his right. They were cut off on both flanks, and he was forced to redirect his path to the south toward a parking structure on High Street, a football field's length away.

Rocks and hunks of concrete pelted his back as he struggled under his friend's weight. He heard the clunks of heavy objects striking Vasquez's riot shield. Both spurred him forward. He stretched his left hand behind him, firing pepper balls wildly to slow the fast-moving mob. The action enraging the anarchists as they surged through the pain-inducing chemical.

Mathews willed his legs to move, praying he didn't trip on the debris-littered street. As he crested the curb in front of the parking garage, the force of a brick slamming into his left leg knocked him to the ground.

The beleaguered officer scrambled to a seated position in front of Vasquez, trying to protect the unconscious man. Desperate to buy them a few more seconds, he reached for his backup weapon strapped to his ankle. The Smith & Wesson Body Guard held a meager six .380 hollow-point rounds. But it was something. Maybe it would slow the mob down. Where the fuck was their backup?

He dropped the Body Guard's sights onto the forehead of a man at the leading edge of the mob. At this distance, and with the pistol's heavy trigger pull, the chances of hitting his target were nil.

He applied more pressure to the trigger. The thought of taking a life forced a scream from his fear-dried throat. "This doesn't have to happen. Please, STOP!"

At the end of the trigger stroke, the swarm of humanity disappeared behind a desert-tan armored personnel carrier as it rumbled to a stop between them. Mathews released the tension on the trigger, relief flooding his body before being replaced by a fresh wave of panic. "Vasquez!" He pivoted to face his partner. "Wake up. You've got to wake up."

Vasquez's blood-crusted eyelids fluttered.

"I need some help. Someone help me get him into the APC!" Mathews screamed while inspecting the ragged gash on his friend's forehead.

Mathews turned as the sound of boots slapping pavement reached him. He expected to see soldiers brawling with rioters while others made their way to help him with Vasquez. What he found confused his adrenaline-addled mind.

Soldiers in full battle-rattle faced a subdued gathering of his former combatants. People who were cheering for his death only seconds ago were now docile as they milled about like factory workers waiting for the whistle to blow, signaling the end of their shift. No screaming rage or calls for Mathews' death. Only indifference.

More importantly, no one moved to help Vasquez.

"Hey! I need some help."

His sharp tone grabbed the attention of a soldier exiting the APC with a large medical kit slung over her shoulder. The women's hard eyes met his, then drifted to his downed partner. The sight of Vasquez's blood-streaked face raised her eyebrows as she rushed to help.

"What happened to him?" she asked while tearing open a package of gauze.

"He took a brick to the head. His eyes opened a second ago, but I can't get him to wake up. He needs a hospital, now!"

The soldier ignored his proclamation, focusing on cleaning and dressing Vasquez's wound. "Why isn't he wearing a riot helmet." She glared at him. "Why aren't you?"

Mathews' anger flared at the question. "Orders came down that we were to look less like an invading military force." He looked back to his friend and asked, "Is he going to be okay? His wife is pregnant."

"Sir, I'm doing everything I can right now. But you have to let me work."

Mathews, no stranger to how battlefield medics operated, obeyed by standing on shaky legs and walking towards a soldier wearing sergeant stripes on his Army Combat Uniform's sleeve. "You the CO?"

The older man spun to face Mathews, relief spreading over his face when he realized a peaceful protester hadn't broken through their defensive perimeter. "Yes, I'm Sergeant Adams. Who are you?"

"Sergeant Adams, I'm Officer Mathews. That's my partner your medic is working on. You and your squad just saved our lives. Thank you."

A quizzical look flashed on the sergeant's face. "I didn't think... Never mind. You're welcome." He kept his gaze on Mathews then asked, "Anything else, Officer Mathews?"

Mathews broke his stare and glanced at the crowd that was retreating to East Fourth Street. "I do. What the hell just happened? I mean, just a few minutes ago, they were trying to kill us, execute both of us. You guys show up, and they turn as tame as a flock of sheep. It's not their MO. One more thing. Why send regular Army and not the National Guard? Seems a bit overkill-ish."

"You'd have to ask that group," Sergeant Adams growled while pointing at the group in question. "Why they're acting like *sheep*. The National Guard will relieve us after they're vetted."

"Vetted?" Mathews began. "Vetted for what? Doesn't that happen *before* they join the Guard?"

Sergeant Adams took a hard step towards him with balled fists. Mathews knew what came next if he pressed his interrogation. "Easy, Sarge, we're on the same team, I think. Getting my partner to a hospital is the only thing that matters."

The squad medic interrupted the surreal conversation. "Sergeant, this man needs a hospital A-SAP!"

***

Mathews exited the squad car and said his goodbyes to his commander. No 10-7 radio call or farewell party, and no smiling faces. His career simply ended when the door to the cruiser slammed shut. He was no longer a police officer.

The sun was bright in the late morning sky as he walked slowly up his driveway, thoughts of Vasquez weighing heavy on his mind. He'd suffered intracranial pressure or, simply put, brain swelling. The surgeon removed a section of his skull and inserted a drain tube to ease the pressure. The doctors wouldn't know the long-term effect on his brain function for several days.

He'd stayed at the hospital until the doctors got Vasquez stabilized and the young man's wife settled down. Telling her what had happened was the hardest thing he'd done in his twenty-seven years on the force. The accusation in her eyes crushed him.

But something else was eating at him. The conversation he'd had with the medic during the frantic ride to Saint Vincent's Hospital. He had asked her the same question he'd asked Sergeant Adams. Why did the mob stop rioting when the APC arrived? Her cryptic, non-answer threw him: *It's what they're supposed to do.* Unable to wrench more detail from her, he stored the comment away. *I'll be looking into that*, he thought as the APC slammed to a stop under the ambulance-offloading pavilion.

Mathews was two steps from his front door when he heard it. The telltale screeching of his neighbors' screen door as it swung open. His back went stiff. *Not today*, he thought as he quickened his step to make it into his home before his neighbors reached the property line.

"Scurry, scurry, little pig. But you're not fast enough. I'm here to remind you *pigs* get no rest."

Mathews ignored Thatcher's taunt and slid his house key into the deadbolt.

"Where's your Latino servant who usually drives his master to-and-fro? Did you leave him tied to the whipping post?"

Mathews abruptly faced Thatcher, the action causing the stick man to flinch. Letting his duty belt fall to the porch, he was moving at Thatcher on instinct.

He was mere steps away from the property line when a loud bang sounded from the neighbor's house on the other side of Thatcher's, causing the man to scramble to escape the unseen threat sneaking up behind him. When Thatcher bounced off Mathews' broad chest, he yelped and twirled, his flailing right arm slamming into Mathews' face.

Recovering from the blow quickly, Mathews grabbed Thatcher's throat and pulled him nose to nose. He asked loudly enough to be recorded by Thatcher's ever-present iPhone, "Why did you attack me? I didn't say a word to you. You came onto my property and attacked me. I feared for my life. You left me no choice but to defend myself."

The air rushed from Thatcher's lungs when his back slammed to the cold, damp earth. His vision went hazy as he struggled to force air through Mathews' vice-like grip. It was hopeless. The man was too powerful. Desperate, he slapped and pushed at Mathews' face, but he held fast to Thatcher's neck.

Shadows seeped around the corners of his vision as resignation set in and his arms fell to his sides. His wife's distant screams reached through the fog, but he held no hope she'd save him.

As unconsciousness wrapped its dark arms around him, Mathews' hand disappeared from his neck. Rolling to his side, he gulped air as he clawed at the ground, trying to escape to safety. His wife appeared at his side a moment later, attempting to drag him away from Mathews.

As Thatcher recovered, he became aware of two shapes hovering above him, their sudden appearance reigniting his panic. He clawed and kicked at the ground as Margaux pulled on his shirt.

Once safely back on his property, he got to his knees but lacked the strength to stand. Margaux continued pulling on his shirt, desperate to get him into their home. He slapped her hand from his flannel.

Roaring laughter pulled his attention back to the hulking forms. Vision clearing, he recognized Mathews immediately. A second clicked by before he determined who the other person was.

Willis Stinger stood next to Mathews, both men still in hysterics. Thatcher suddenly found his voice. "I'm calling the police. I'll have your badge by the end of the day."

The proclamation elicited more laughter from Mathews, and he responded through gasps for air, "I'll give it to you myself."

Thatcher struggled to his feet, again batting away his wife's efforts to drag him to safety. "Margaux, dial 911. Inform them one of their own is guilty of attempted murder of an innocent civilian, and we captured it on video."

Willis' posture went serious as he locked eyes with Thatcher while addressing his wife. "You do that, Margaux. I'll be sure to show them my video as well. It's time for you to consider the penalty for filing a false police report."

***

Twenty minutes later, Mathews handed Willis a beer as the men took a seat at his kitchen table. "Thanks again for pulling me off that little prick. I'd lost control, I'm not sure...."

Willis smiled, took a long pull from the bottle, and said, "Least I could do considering it was me that scared him onto your property. But Jesus H, I didn't expect him to take a swing at you."

"That's the problem with Marines; you guys never think things through," Mathews said through a crooked smile.

Willis burst into laughter. "That's funny, coming from a former Green Machine grunt. You guys couldn't tie your shoes without our help."

The former military men continued their lighthearted ribbing for a while before falling into a more serious conversation about the state of American politics. Mathews filled Willis in on the violence exploding downtown and what had happened to his partner.

The mention of Vasquez prompted Mathews to call Saint Vincent's and check the young man's condition. No change.

After a couple of minutes, Willis asked, "You notice that plumbing van parked out front? It hasn't moved in a couple of months. I don't recall any plumbers living in our neighborhood, do you?"

Mathews gave him a knowing look. "I have. I tried looking through its windows, see what I could see. But the rear windows are blacked out. The cab is spotless, not what you'd expect. I ran the license; it came back registered to a leasing company."

Willis hitched his eyebrows as he leaned close to Mathews. "Turn your radio on. We need to talk."

CHAPTER 22

JACK AND LISA'S HOME

Jack canceled their trip downtown after Lisa checked the Rock & Roll Hall of Fame's website and found it was closed due to civil unrest. When they'd planned their visit to the Hall, they'd been aware of what the local media framed as "peaceful protests and isolated violence," but they'd seen no news coverage of major riots.

Lisa surfed YouTube for videos of the alleged *civil unrest*, finding only "Video Removed" messages. When she tried searching several alternate video sharing platforms, her web browser returned a "404 Page Not Found" error. She found an abundance of videos depicting peaceful marches supporting gun control but not a hint of violent protests.

Jack was fine with the change in plans. His unexpected trip to UW's house had lasted into the early morning, and frankly, he was looking forward to a Sunday of doing nothing. But Lisa's research into the reason their plans were upended changed the trajectory of their day.

She'd been mildly annoyed when her social media pages went dark. Today, she was livid about it. She called some friends to see if they knew anything about riots. One of her friends, who worked downtown, told her what he'd witnessed and confirmed that the unrest had been widespread and extremely violent.

Jack's head was still spinning from the information UW had shared with him. He decided not to share it with Lisa. They had enough trouble in their lives. Tossing in his uncle's rants about tyrannical government seemed a bad idea.

But when she found him stretched out on the couch, he realized she'd put the puzzle together on her own. He'd been sharing the story of his visit with UW ever since.

Lisa had Jack locked in her sights. "So, what you're telling me is a third of our military has been unceremoniously discharged from active duty?"

Jack nodded.

"And Eden's administration hasn't finished interviewing them?"

Another affirming nod from Jack.

"And now they're talking about federalizing the National Guard?"

"After they finish reviewing the enlisted, they'll review the National Guard. And yes, then they plan to federalize them," Jack elaborated.

Lisa's shock was obvious. She understood what it all meant. But Jack tried to resist getting caught up in speculation. He remained unwavering in his belief in America's political system, that they had the power to turn this around in November.

"Jack, don't take offense, but get your head out of your ass. Eden is moving to seize control. And to do that, he needs to ensure our military stands down. He's molding them into a compliant puppet, his personal army. Don't you see that, Jack? This cannot end well for the country."

Jack's stomach dropped. To hear his extremely sensible wife repeat UW's words verbatim sent anxiety rushing through his body. "Head out of my ass? How am I not supposed to take offense to that?" Jack didn't wait for Lisa's answer. "I still think we can turn it around. The midterms are around the corner. I'm confident we'll take both chambers back in November."

"Jack, I love your optimism, always have. But it all became crystal-clear for me today. What they've done to us, to Stinger Machinery, and now the military all means one thing. Eden wants control over every aspect of our lives. He's using the *crisis* to shut us down, to weaken us. We've already been cut off from Chirp and Friend Me; I can't get a single alternative social media site to load, and they control the flow of information through a submissive media. How else can you explain why we didn't know how bad things were downtown? Mark my words, Uncle Willis was right. They'll come for our guns next. And, so what if we take back the House and Senate? The idiots we voted for have been useless."

They stood staring silently at one another, Jack struggling with the reality she'd presented, Lisa struggling with why her husband couldn't see the truth in her words. Jack felt his chest tightening. He had to get some fresh air before he passed out.

Head spinning, he moved towards the front door. This couldn't be happening; his wife was as crazy as his uncle! "I'm taking a walk. I'll try to figure out how to get my HEAD OUT OF MY ASS. And you should rethink what you said. Every word. You're talking about the United States government attempting to subvert its own people. It's crazy, Lisa. Eden's a train wreck, and he's ignoring the Constitution… sure. But overthrow the country? Never happen. It's crazy talk."

Jack's harsh tone caught Lisa off guard. It didn't change her mind, but she wasn't used to him losing his temper. He was emotionally rock solid, always even-keeled. At that moment, Lisa realized the toll the stress of the last year had taken. But he needed to understand, to stop being naïve, so blind to what was happening around him.

"I will, Jack. But answer a question. When will the business start paying you again? Probably after it defaults on the government loan, they take control, and you become the manager instead of the owner?"

Lisa's statement rocked Jack. She knew more about Stinger Machinery's financial trouble than he'd realized. He felt his anger build, anger about so many different things. Foremost was his anger at losing control of his world. His trust in a system he believed in was shattered.

He stormed through the front door and into the chilled February air, trying to regain control over his emotions, to sort through his thoughts. He had to rationalize what his wife and UW were telling him, what they were thinking. He feared they were right.

CHAPTER 23

JACK AND LISA'S HOME

His anger dulled only slightly, Jack was forced home an hour after he started his walk, the plummeting temperature too painful to ignore. He could have walked the streets for the entire night had he not forgotten his jacket.

He paused before pushing back into the house, readying himself for the argument that had forced him into the streets to restart. Pulling a deep, calming breath, he pushed open the front door and embraced the warmth of his home.

Lisa sat on the couch, facing the darkened television. She turned to him and held out the remote control. "You need to watch something; I recorded it for you, on the DVR. I'll be upstairs. When you finish, we can talk."

Not sure what to make of Lisa's puzzling request, Jack tried to apologize, but she cut him off. "Just watch what I recorded for you. I'll be waiting upstairs."

When he didn't respond, she set the remote on the coffee table and walked towards the stairs. As Jack watched the love of his life disappear up the darkened staircase, he grew worried about what the video would tell him. Was it a farewell video from Lisa? He quickly banished the thought. She said it was DVR'ed. Meaning it couldn't be a personal message from her.

Torn between following his wife and watching the video, he chose the latter, surmising it would allot him more time to work through his emotions.

Jack plopped onto the couch and powered on the television, then navigated through the DVR menu until he found the most recent recording. He noted the recording's title, *Emergency Broadcast*, and it sent a chill down his spine.

Jack watched disbelievingly as Vice President Genus addressed the nation, not President Eden. But Eden's absence was only the beginning. The message delivered was devastating.

By the time Genus finished her broadcast, dozens of inalienable rights had disappeared, and Jack had learned a new phrase: "Essential workers in essential industries." She'd proffered no insight as to what that phrase encompassed, only promising a list of *essentials* would soon follow.

The message, however, was clear. The movements of the United States' populace would be restricted to crucial activities only. His government's intent was to enforce this order by deploying the military in coordination with local law enforcement and, at a later date, the National Guard.

The threat to personal safety is too great was the oft-repeated message. "I'm from the government, and I'm here to help," Jack whispered as Genus pushed on.

He had no sooner asked himself why, suddenly, it had become too dangerous for the average person to leave their home when Genus answered his question.

"As you're aware, or should be," she said, her cackling laugh interrupting the message. "Millions have taken to the streets to peacefully protest in support of so many virtuous causes. They have shown us that America no longer *wants* an armed society, will no longer *tolerate* corporate greed. They are demanding an equitable system. A system that lifts all of us to the beauty of equivalence, of unity."

Genus stared into the camera for a long uncomfortable thirty seconds. Seeming both enamored with her own self-righteousness and hopelessly confused, she glanced to a point off-camera, nodded her head, and re-launched her diatribe. "Unfortunately, violent domestic terrorists have infiltrated these groups, leveling the same violence against the activists and cities in which they are peacefully protesting as they have against your government officials. Make no mistake: These extremists are your neighbors, friends, and family. They walk among you every day. It is for that reason we are declaring nationwide martial law effective at midnight tomorrow. This should allow each of you ample time to secure groceries, retrieve items from your places of employment, and check on loved ones."

Again she paused, searching for direction from an unknown source off-camera. "Oh, yes, yes," she started, then, realizing she was still broadcasting, morphed back into the role of concerned parent. "If your business or occupation is classified as essential, you are required to fill out a Form 85REM-Request for Essential Movement. The form will be mailed to you upon request. If approved, a badge identifying you as essential will be delivered to you. Badges must be displayed at all times when traveling outside of your home."

Thunderstruck, Jack bolted from the couch, leaving Genus babbling to an empty room. He rushed upstairs, heading to their home office, and found Lisa hunched over their laptop. She met his panicked gaze.

"Jack, I can't log in."

"Whatever it is can wait. We need to access our investment account. The markets are going to tank. We need to either move our money, or cash out," Jack countered while hurrying around the desk.

"That's what I'm talking about, Jack. I can't log in to our Fidelity account."

Incredulous, he pushed past Lisa to gain control over the laptop. His knees went soft as he read the message: "Access Denied. Please submit Form 85IAA-Investment Account Access to the Bureau of Financial Equity. Upon approval, your account privileges will be restored."

Jack's mind switched to more immediate matters. "Get dressed; we're going to the store."

***

Jack turned their SUV into the Super Centers parking lot and slammed to a stop only a few feet off the main road. They faced utter chaos. Hundreds of people stood in lines stretching the length of the acres-long blacktop surface to enter the store. Fights among the frantic masses raged unchecked throughout the parking lot.

Lisa's startled gasp yanked Jack's attention to her. His gaze followed her outstretched finger to the military vehicles and armed soldiers guarding the store's entrance. As he watched, he realized they were controlling access. As one shopper exited the store, another was granted entry.

A body slamming into his Yukon pulled his attention to its front passenger-side quarter panel. The action was quickly followed by shouted death threats from unseen combatants.

"Get us out of here!" Lisa's voice was nine octaves higher than normal.

Jack had already shifted into reverse, but he found the path behind him blocked by at least three cars. One sat abandoned by its owners as they scrambled to join the ever-growing line of desperate people attempting to enter the store.

"Oh God," Lisa screamed while ducking under the dashboard. "GUN."

Jack whipped his head in her direction and found the crowd to their side had grown exponentially in the seconds he'd been staring in his side-view mirror. A dozen bodies were now tangled together, engaged in mortal combat over a shopping cart full of groceries.

Jack yelled to Lisa to stay down. He'd have to clear a path using the Yukon as a battering ram. He slammed the monster into Reverse and smashed the gas pedal. Fuel ignited the powerful 6.2-liter engine as it hurled the oversized beast toward the cluster of cars blocking their escape.

The impact jolted Lisa against the seats and wrenched Jack's hands from the steering wheel, but he kept the pedal pinned to the floor. A subcompact was first to fall victim to the Yukon's assault and bounced violently to the right, pulling a second car with it. The resulting path was just large enough for Jack to snake through and reach the street fronting the Super Center.

He slammed the transmission into Drive and accelerated away from the store, leaving the irate owners of crumpled cars behind.

"It's okay. You can sit up now," he told Lisa.

When she rose, Jack noticed a glint in her right hand. Her gun, clutched tightly and ready. His wife was obviously prepared to defend them; he had forgotten his gun. A mistake Jack realized he could never make again.

He glanced at his wife as they passed the ever-increasing line of cars trying to enter the Super Center's parking lot. Noting the hard set to her jaw, he reached over and placed his hand on her leg reassuringly.

She turned her gaze to him. "It's unraveling, and it's just the beginning."

Jack wanted to console her, tell her the situation wouldn't last, but he'd be lying.

His phone buzzed to life a few seconds later. UW was calling.

"Are you two safe?" he asked, concern straining his voice while the ever-present radio blared in the background.

"We are now!" Jack paused, attempting to calm his nerves. "Did you know this was coming? Jesus, UW, martial law? Nationwide? How does a society function while locked away in their homes?" His questions came rapid-fire.

"Slow down, Jack. I knew the military was deploying. But I wasn't told why. The protests distracted everyone." UW paused, then said, "Looks like you're beginning to understand, to see things more clearly. When you come over to pick up food, bring Lisa. We'll talk, and I'll be introducing you to a friend. I'll see you in thirty."

Chapter 24

Willis Stinger's Home

Jack strained to hear UW over the blaring radio. Sweat beaded along his hairline. *My family has gone mad.* The thought banged around his mind, causing a headache that threatened to split his skull.

He surveyed the basement space his uncle had corralled them into. It had been several years since Jack was last in the basement. Since then, UW had remodeled it into a study. It now sported dark-wood paneling with massive bookshelves flanking the group on three sides. They sat in leather chairs surrounding a small, well-stocked bar anchoring the study's far wall. But Jack recalled the area being larger when last he saw it. He couldn't be positive, but he remembered a sizable workshop along with other nooks and crannies usually found in the basements of older homes. Gone too were the undersized ground-level basement windows. Elements that had added a sense of openness. Now, it felt mildly claustrophobic.

Jack was examining the bookcases when something UW said grabbed his attention.

"Color-coded non-essential person passes start mailing out in two weeks. BHR and BCR are using snail mail to deliver them to three hundred million people. Think about that. It'll be weeks, maybe months, before they arrive. Until you receive your pass, you'll only be allowed to go to the grocery store, your doctor's appointments, or whatever else the government deems essential, on assigned days, alphabetically by last name. Mark my words, the only way to enforce that is with military checkpoints stopping every single car and person found in public. They will flood our streets with armed soldiers."

"Wait, what?" Jack interjected. "Non-essential person passes, shopping alphabetically? Like during the '70s gas crisis when you fueled up based on your license plate? Who told you that, UW? Genus mentioned nothing about passes or alphabets."

UW regarded him for a long minute before speaking. "Jack, did you watch the entire broadcast?"

Jack's brow hitched in surprise. "I thought I did. I got to the part about essential passes. What else did she say?"

All eyes focused on UW as he filled Jack in on the rest of Genus' speech. He took special care to make clear the part covering non-essentials and the limits placed on their movements. It sounded like house arrest to Jack. They were even dictating the distance people could travel from their front doors while in their own yard. They had to remain a minimum of ten feet from the street and their property lines. The results would be complete isolation from their neighbors.

"They cannot do that!" Jack blurted out.

"Well, Jack. They just did. My suggestion is that you and Lisa go home, pack up anything important, and stay with me. Our government is always quick to take; it's never quick to give back."

"I agree," Lisa answered before Jack had even registered UW's words. "Strength in numbers."

"Whoa, hold on. I'm not moving out of my home. That's crazy. This isn't Nazi Germany. We still have rights," Jack countered.

"You're right, Jack. We're not in Germany. But our government sure is starting to resemble the Nazi party."

Jack looked over at the man he'd just met. Mathews had been quiet during most of the conversation, only speaking when telling the story about what had happened downtown and the unsettling actions of the rioters when they encountered the military. The words *like it was planned* nibbled at Jack's mind.

He shoved the thoughts away; they were all acting like crazy paranoid nut jobs. And it was rubbing off on him. Jack stood. He'd heard enough. "The government isn't trying to enslave us. Is it guilty of unforgivable overreach? Yes. But what do they gain by turning everyday citizens into slaves?" He met the stares of each person in the room. "It makes no sense. I refuse to believe that's their goal. Now, Lisa and I are going home."

"Jack," Lisa interrupted, "I'm staying here. At least until things settle down." Her tone, one Jack was familiar with, left no question. Her decision was final.

Tossing his hands in the air in frustration, he stormed towards the stairs to escape the madness. As he traversed the small study, he yelled over his shoulder, "You're wasting time and effort. We should be talking to our friends and neighbors, convincing them to vote this administration out of existence."

UW's words reached him as he arrived at the staircase. "How do you suppose we do that, Jack? Our government has made it illegal for us to be outside of our homes without permission.

They have saddled us with a national state of emergency, a public health emergency, and now we live under martial law. Each removed freedoms, each designed to induce fear."

UW's statement stung him with truth, stopping him mid-step. His mind was at war with the reality unfolding around him. "I'll find a way!"

"Jack, consider this. Rye's assassin was estimated to have been a mile away. Only a handful of snipers worldwide can make that shot. Who possesses the means to find them? Who has the power to employ them? Now, consider that seven other officials suffered the same fate. Who's responsible, Jack?"

Jack didn't answer. Doing so would mean acknowledging a truth he was unable to accept. Instead, he quickened his pace, desperate to separate himself from people he no longer recognized.

Chapter 25

Thirteen Months Post Inauguration, Fleming's Grocery Store

Standing in an hour's-long line to enter the grocery store now resembled a walk through a daisy field in full bloom. Once inside the store, he realized how bad things had gotten.

He'd passed on his first assigned shopping day, two weeks ago, thinking they would lift the restrictions in a matter of days. A sign informing him the store was closed due to a lack of inventory had abbreviated his second assigned shopping day. When Jack left home at the crack of dawn this morning, he decided he'd buy everything he could lay his hands on. But what greeted him was a sea of humanity with a shared mindset, forcing their way past other shoppers only to find empty shelves. People ripped items from other shoppers' carts as fist fights and screaming matches raged throughout the store.

Every item had a purchase limit of one, but it didn't matter because every shelf appeared to be empty. Jack rushed to the canned goods first and found a blood-smeared floor beneath an empty shelving gondola. He couldn't be sure, but he thought he saw human teeth resting in the puddle of blood oozing its way toward his cart's front wheels.

Anxiety blossoming in his gut, he whipped his cart around and broke into a full-out run towards the dry goods section. A fresh supply of boxed noodles sat atop a pallet as a stockboy cowered against its contents. Frenzied people reached past the teenager, throwing anything they could reach into their carts.

Jack realized this might be his last opportunity to secure any food today and for the days ahead. He lowered his shoulder, shut his eyes, and plunged headlong into the fray, ignoring the angry shouts of those he barreled into. He knew he had reached the pallet when his shoulder slammed against a cardboard box full of angel hair pasta. He twisted his body to face the box and wrenched it free. As he turned to escape the madness, he came nose to nose with the stock boy's terrified, tear-streaked face.

"Grab hold of my shirt and don't stop for anything," he screamed at the young man.

The boy latched onto Jack and buried his face in his back as he plowed through the crowd. As they broke through the mayhem, the sobbing teen bolted from the area and headed towards the safety of the store's back room.

After making sure the stockboy made it through the large double doors, Jack slammed his prize into the metal cart's child seat, draped his arm over it, and sprinted towards the checkouts.

An armed National Guardsman stood watch over the hundreds of people desperate to end this nightmare. Once Jack made it inside the steel crowd-control barriers, he relaxed but kept his arm over the case of noodles.

He realized he now viewed every person standing in line with him as a potential threat. Each person was as desperate as him. Each person held the potential for violence justified by the need to feed themselves and their families.

He let his gaze wander around the crowded space. As each person avoided making eye contact, he understood they viewed him the same as he did them. A threat. He noticed more than a dozen men with oversized shirts covering angular bulges at their hips. Knowing what that meant, he adjusted his IWB holster, realizing the six rounds in his Ruger LCP would be practically useless if a full-blown gun fight broke out. With his other guns locked away in UW's gun safe, the LCP was his primary carry option. Something he'd need to change.

As he snaked through the metal barrier, edging closer to the checkout, the armed guards positioned at each register came into view. They weren't of the "rent a cop" variety—they were hard-looking men and women in black tactical uniforms, each sporting an insignia patch identifying them as BHR troops. *When did the Bureau of Harm Reduction go full military?* he mused.

Jack was next in line when suddenly the cashier barked at the woman ahead of him, "You have too much stuff. Pick what you need and leave the rest behind. You're allowed one of each item only."

The woman began pleading with the cashier. Begging her to make an exception, saying something about three children to feed. Unfazed, the cashier nodded to the BHR enforcer standing to her right. What happened next made Jack's teeth grind together with anger.

The enforcer quick-stepped around the checkout and wrenched the cart from the now-hysterical woman's grasp. He quickly slammed the items on the conveyor belt back into her shopping cart and pushed it into the exit aisle, where another BHR enforcer whisked it away.

As Jack watched the gut-wrenching drama unfold in front of him, he realized he would soon suffer the same fate as the sobbing woman begging for a second chance while the BHR dragged her kicking and screaming to the exit.

The cashier's smug look told Jack she was reveling in the power she wielded over the desperate shoppers. She waited until her assigned BHR guard returned to his station before turning her attention to Jack.

He caught the hint of a smile as she eyed the contents of his shopping cart. *You're enjoying this*, he thought. As he placed the case of noodles atop the conveyor, the cashier whispered something to the BHR guard, causing a similar grin to crease his features.

"YOU HAVE TOO MUCH STUFF," she bellowed.

"It's all I could find. Your store is a war-zone, you know that, right?"

Unfazed, she said, "YOU HAVE TOO MUCH STUFF. EVERYTHING HAS A ONE-ITEM LIMIT!"

Jack caught a flash of movement behind the cashier and assumed the BHR guard was moving to confiscate his meager supplies. It surprised him to see the young stockboy he'd rescued from the angry mob. He leaned in close and whispered in the woman's ear. Her head dipped in understanding as she passed the message along to the guard.

With a nod, she said, just above a whisper, "Today, and only today, I'll make an exception."

Relief spread over Jack, and he instantly understood the power of fear. He knew, from this point forward, the government would use it to keep the masses obedient.

He tried to thank the youngster, but he'd vanished as quickly as he'd appeared.

After paying three times the normal price for his meager haul, Jack leaned over the counter, causing the woman to flinch, and said, "You know they're not on your side." He nodded towards the guard. "One day, you'll be that woman you just sicced your dog on."

He quickly exited the store before the woman could change her mind and jogged to his Yukon, on high alert to avoid the thugs roving the parking lot, searching for easy prey.

***

Jack exited the grocery store's parking lot and headed for Stinger Machinery. It was a risky move considering his shopping privileges only allowed him to secure *essential* supplies. He could be arrested, fined, or who knows what, if caught. But his request for essential business status had gone unanswered. Calls and voicemails to Agent Woods had also gone unreturned, and his House and Senate reps were missing in action. Stinger Machinery would be forced to close its doors permanently if they denied his essential status request. But no one seemed to care.

His intent was to check on the building, make sure it was still standing, and return home. As he turned onto the access road leading to Stinger Machinery, his phone buzzed. Lisa was calling. He answered the call through the Yukon's Bluetooth connection. "Have you tried to go grocery shopping?" he blurted out.

"Hello to you too, Jack," Lisa responded. "And no, I haven't. UW's stores of canned and emergency food should last a few more months. I'm guessing your trip didn't go well?"

Jack bristled. It had been two weeks, and she still refused to come home. The strain on their relationship from her bullheadedness was growing. "Good for you," he started, "and no, it didn't. Insane is a better description. I'm going to check on the business, make sure it's still standing."

They were quiet for a moment before Jack spoke. "Are you coming home? I miss you."

Lisa's reply went unheard as Jack pulled into Stinger's parking lot, his attention drawn to the light burning in his office window. "Why are the lights on?" he blurted, cutting Lisa off. "I have to go. Something's wrong."

"What? What's wrong, Jack?"

"I need to go. I'll call you back," he said as he disconnected the call.

He was bursting into the building before he realized he'd even left the Yukon. Hand resting on his Ruger, he stopped hard when an unfamiliar face greeted him from behind the reception desk. The woman's face was unfamiliar, but her uniform wasn't. Gray sports coat over a heavily starched white dress shirt.

"Who the fuck are you? Why are you here?" he shouted.

A door slamming to his left caused Jack to turn towards the area where his office was located. The self-righteous BHR Observer stood in front of the door, blocking Jack's access.

"What's going on?" Jack shouted.

"It's good to see you again, Mister Stinger. I apologize for the confusion. It seems the Bureau of Harm Reduction's timing when switching all communication to standard mail delivery was, shall we say, *poor*."

"What are you talking about? Answer my question!"

"Mister Stinger, I don't possess the proper credentials to answer your question. You should contact Agent Woods. She'll be able to explain."

Jack lost control. Consumed with anger, he rushed the BHR Observer and pinned him to the wall, his forearm pressed firmly on the man's throat. "This is my business; you have no right to be here. You're trespassing," he screamed, inches from the terrified man's face.

Gasping for air, the Observer wheezed through his response, "Call Agent Woods."

Jack removed his forearm from the Observer's throat and shoved the wisp of a man towards the exit. "Get out."

Not waiting to see if the BHR Observer followed his order, Jack stormed through the door separating the reception area from the offices. His confusion deepened when he gazed upon the frightened faces of a half-dozen strangers occupying the space.

"All of you get your gray-suit-wearing asses out of my business. NOW!"

When the group remained huddled together, he stutter-stepped in their direction, causing them to scurry like rats for the exit.

He turned in a circle, searching for stragglers, when suddenly the sound of grinding metal reached his ears. Panic overpowered his anger as realization took root. He barreled into the machine shop and pulled a sharp breath. Half of Stinger Machinery's equipment was running at full-bore and manned by strangers.

He quickly identified the grinding as coming from his new CNC machine. He ran to the machine and found smoke billowing from its cutting head. Jack shoved the inept operator from the controls, pulled open the kill switch's molly-guard, and slammed his hand on it, cutting the machine's power.

He turned toward the stunned operator and grabbed him by the collar of his gray coveralls. "Get out of my shop," he barked while shoving the man towards the exit. "This is my business; none of you belong here."

His actions had drawn the attention of the other *machinists*, who began powering down their machines and stalking in Jack's direction as he ordered them to leave.

A filth-covered man sporting a long scraggly beard squinted at Jack. "This is a union shop, pal. And you're inside the yellow tape," he said while bobbing his head at the floor. "Non-machinist employees are to remain outside the tapeline."

The group continued their menacing approach. Jack squared off, inviting them to receive the ass-kicking of a lifetime. "You're about to make a huge mistake," he growled.

The group's leader hard-stepped in Jack's direction at the same instant the shop door burst open and a police officer rushed into the room. "Everyone needs to calm down," he shouted as he took a position between Jack and the machinists.

Neither side made a move now that the officer stood between them. He glared at both sides and said, "I think it's safe to say the workday has ended. Everyone, go home, cool off, and start fresh tomorrow. You boys," he said, nodding towards the machinists, "head out now. You," Jack received the nod this time, "wait here until they're gone."

The tension in Jack's posture eased as the machinists headed for the exit, seemingly happy with the unexpected early quitting time. They avoided eye contact with Jack as they grumbled empty boasts of what would have happened to Jack if the police hadn't arrived.

As the motley crew slammed the door behind them, the police officer faced Jack. "Mister Stinger, I presume?"

"How do you know my name? Who called the police?" Jack asked suspiciously.

"A friend of your uncle sent me."

CHAPTER 26

MOUNT WEATHER EMERGENCY OPERATIONS CENTER

Chief of Staff Roberts stared blankly at the enormous monitors mounted on the walls of the conference room buried deep inside Mount Weather's EOC. They displayed the scowling faces of fifty Congressmen and women, and Roberts decided he hated all of them.

The briefings were held in groups of fifty until all five hundred and thirty-five miserable members received their opportunity at five minutes of useless pontification.

They had forced him to brief Congress after Genus' national address and subsequent Martial Law declaration. Roberts had anticipated the uproar and how it would play out. He would suffer through while blustering windbags demanded personal meetings with Eden, threatened legal action, and complained about the BHR's heavy-handed enforcement at the local level. And he wasn't disappointed. Annoyed, tired, and bored, but not disappointed.

Currently, Republican Senator Rodman, from Ohio, held the floor. "Our supply chain shattered in a matter of hours, Roberts. Not days or weeks, hours. Food production and deliveries have ground to a halt. Riots are breaking out at stores across the country.

The nation was unprepared for Eden's complete shutdown." The senator paused while glaring at Roberts, then branched into a topic Roberts hadn't prepared for. "Furthermore, hundreds of thousands of people remain stranded in hotels throughout the country and across the globe. They're unable to secure safe passage home because of Eden's questionable actions. How does he plan to rectify that situation?"

The question startled Roberts. He'd never considered Americans would be in other countries, free of government control. A situation he planned to remedy immediately.

As he jotted a note about the situation into his planner, the senator decided he hadn't finished. "Why the hell did Genus deliver this news? Where is Eden? I expected to see his blank stare, not yours! And don't you dare tell me his absence is a safety protocol. I've visited Mount Weather; a fly can't enter that facility without a full cavity search."

Roberts fidgeted uncomfortably; the senator had latched on with pit-bull tenacity. "As I have already stated, President Eden is unwell this morning and sends his regrets. Now, about the stranded…"

"You're lying!" Rodman interrupted. "Eden would've made this meeting if he were on his deathbed. I've never liked the man, but I've worked with him for over thirty years. He always shows up for work, especially during national emergencies. Now, we're going to give you until tomorrow to arrange a meeting with our inept Commander-in-Chief. If not, I'll speak with the governor of Ohio. I'll tell him to pull the National Guard back, to disregard the administration's orders, open every business, every school… everything. Because my instincts tell me this isn't about public safety. It's about control."

Roberts bristled at Senator Rodman's rebuke. But he was too rattled that the sharp-elbowed politician had already put the puzzle together to offer a sufficient retort.

Instead, he stumbled through feigned dismay. "Senator Roberts, although I understand your emotional state, your inference of ulterior motives is deeply insulting. The administration's actions are driven purely by the desire to keep the American people safe. Need I remind you that *seven* government officials lost their lives to these terrorists?"

"I've never doubted or denied that seven officials were assassinated," Rodman interjected, "but as you point out, they were government officials. Not a single civilian life was taken or threatened. Do you know why I doubt your story, Mister Roberts? Because I review the intelligence reports, the same ones you receive. And they detail nothing: no leads, no violent acts, NOTHING. Hell, not a single member of Congress has received even a veiled threat against us or our families. Let alone a threat to public safety!"

The octogenarian breathed heavily into his microphone while holding Roberts in a withering stare. *Now would be a splendid time for your heart to quit pumping blood through your rock-hard arteries,* Roberts thought before Rodman re-launched his diatribe. "How do you explain that? All of those grocery stores with hundreds of people standing, unprotected, in hours'-long lines. And these domestic terrorists, as you're referring to them, haven't attempted one act of violence? They prefer not to wreak havoc on an unarmed, unprotected, and already frightened population? It's preposterous Eden would expect us to believe it to be true."

Roberts waited a breath after Rodman finished. "Senator Rodman, our primary concern is for the safety of Americans across the nation. The lack of violence, or attempts at violence, is a direct result of the administration's swift but difficult choices. I'm sure you can see that simple truth."

Rodman sat back hard in his chair, exasperated by the political *speak*. "You should listen as well as you double-talk; you'd be an unstoppable force if you did. Your administration has cut off every form of social communication possible. Neighbors are reporting one another to your Gestapo-esque BHR and BCR faster than you can print your Form 85PUC Penalty for Unlawful Communication. You've created a nightmarish dystopian reality."

He paused, and Roberts seized the opportunity. "Senator, your five minutes have expired. Please surrender the floor to Senator Burgher."

"I will not! Now, you listen to me. Have Eden pumped full of whatever magic potion you've been mainlining into his feeble brain and ready to talk this time tomorrow. I'm sure I have the full support of every member of Congress in making this demand."

***

Twelve grueling hours later, Roberts stared at the faces of two familiar allies. Gone were the scowling faces of irrelevant politicians who would soon be cast aside in the new government order.

Agent Woods, admittedly his most effective attack dog, flanked Agent Cummings to her right. She was midway through her weekly briefing, although Roberts had heard scarcely little. Lost in the litany of tasks he needed to complete, his attention drifted until Agent Woods cleared her throat, pulling Roberts' attention to the monitor.

"I'm sorry, Agent Woods. I'm a tad distracted. And I'm really not interested in receiving the full report from either of you. However, our business isn't finished. We will be reworking food distribution, nationwide, soon. Your organizations, in conjunction with the National Guard, will be tasked with this monumental responsibility. Begin the procurement process for as many tractor-trailers as possible. Ramp up hiring as well. I'll share more details with you soon, but forward your Form 85PR-Procurement Requests to my office immediately."

Roberts searched his notes until he found what he was looking for. He raised his head as he leaned forward and steepled his fingers. "Do either of your organizations maintain a file on Senator Rodman?"

His question sent both agents pecking away at their keyboards. After a short pause, the agents answered in unison, "We do."

Roberts grinned. "Very good. Forward those files with your Form 85PRs. I want them on my desk by daybreak." Glancing at his watch, he said, "That gives you four hours. Move with haste. Now, if you have nothing further, I'm going to end this call. Agent Cummings, please remain on the line. Agent Woods, dismissed."

The concerned look on Woods' face was exactly the response he desired. *Fear is a powerful tool.* His thought snapped as Woods' video feed faded to black.

Locking an equally concerned Agent Cumming in a hard stare, he asked, "Have you secured additional information on the Bureau of Harm Reduction or its managing agent?"

Relief spread across Cummings' features. "Chief of Staff Roberts, I have. Would you like me to forward it with my other documents?"

"No," Roberts blurted out a little too forcefully. "Use the encrypted email address I supplied you. I'll expect to find it first thing in the morning. Good evening, Agent Cummings."

Roberts disconnected the video feed and glanced around the room, ensuring he was alone. Satisfied, he retrieved his personal cell and selected the only number it ever called. After several rings, a groggy and irritated Rosos answered.

"Mister Rosos, I'm sorry to bother you," Roberts said. "However, we need to *ramp up* in a manner of speaking. I'm sending you an address, one that should receive *special* attention."

Roberts rubbed at his bloodshot eyes as Rosos responded. "Yes, sir. Tomorrow works splendidly. We should have complete control of food distribution by next week. Eden's signature will appear on the Defense Production Act declaration tomorrow, ensuring it happens directly after your actions are carried out. Sir, we get closer every day."

CHAPTER 27

JACK STINGER'S HOME OFFICE

"Yes, I'm sure, Lisa. I'm looking at our account balance as we speak. Only forty-seven thousand dollars remains. Our portfolio has been wiped out."

Jack had intended to call Lisa to have her thank his uncle for intervening at Stinger Machinery, as UW still wasn't answering his calls. He was going to tell her that while the police officer was walking him to his Yukon, he'd received a radio dispatch to respond to an assault on a BHR Observer.

The officer told Jack to *disappear*. "I can't arrest someone I can't find," he'd said before responding to his dispatcher and cutting Jack loose.

But after arriving home, he noticed they'd received their first mail delivery in weeks. Eager to know if he'd been granted essential status, he grabbed the mail and rushed into the house.

His initial shock at finding a sealed, clear plastic bag filled with already opened envelopes was overridden when he noticed the Form 85IAA-Investment Account Access response. With everything going on, he'd forgotten about their investments. Access had been granted.

In his rush to get to his laptop, he overlooked two things. He was *grateful* that the government had granted him access to something he already owned. And a pair of boxes emblazoned with a half-eaten apple rested at the bottom of the plastic bag.

But nothing mattered anymore. They were broke. Millions of dollars—a lifetime of hard work, of scrimping and saving—had evaporated. Raw emotion wrapped his throat in an ever-tightening stranglehold, forcing his words to be spoken between gasps for air.

"We're going to lose everything! Everything we've worked for, Lisa."

Lisa's response, issued in a growling whisper, caught him off guard. "We'll take it back, Jack Stinger. Every red cent. Do you understand me? We're taking it back!"

A click followed by the call being disconnected cut off Jack's reply. Shocked that his wife had hung up on him, he pulled the phone from his ear and prepared to call her back. His breath hitched as he read the message displayed on the phone's screen: "Your service has been disconnected. Our records indicate that your government-issued phone has arrived. Your new phone is set up and ready to use. We've taken the liberty of transferring your contacts and their new government-issued phone numbers to your device. We suggest waiting several days before attempting to call them, as we cannot be sure when everyone will receive their phone. Please discontinue use of your current device immediately. We have loaded a link to in-depth instructions onto your new device. Thank you for your patience during this troublesome time. Your safety is our primary concern. Sincerely, the Bureau of Civic Responsibility."

"Government-issued phone?" Jack blurted.

He shot to his feet and rumbled through his house, heading for the bag of mail he'd thrown to the floor. When he reached it, he knelt and dumped the bag's contents to the floor. He sifted through the heap until his hand struck a hard square box, then a second. The first addressed to him, the second to Lisa.

He realized he was completely cut off from his wife, then remembered that UW still had his landline. He tore open the box to find a phone unlike any he'd ever seen. The gangly hunk of metal and glass more closely resembled a giant Lego than a modern cell phone.

It measured over an inch thick and was roughly nine inches long, reminiscent of the very first mobile phones ever produced. As he lifted it from the box, he realized it tipped the scale at upwards of a pound. He turned it over and saw it had no camera.

He pressed the oversized power button but nothing happened. After pressing and holding it, he realized the battery was dead. Jack scrambled to the kitchen and found the power cord for his current phone. He attempted to connect it to the gov-issued device only to find it was set up for the old-school thirty-pin cable.

"You've got to be shitting me!" he barked.

Rushing back to the box on the floor, he dumped its contents out. With a loud clunk, the needed cord slammed to the floor. He snatched it up and inspected the plug. Considering the government had issued it, he'd expected to find a European-style wall plug but was relieved to find the North American version.

Back in the kitchen, his frustration building, he connected the phone to the charger and waited for the telltale sign of a phone being charged. After a long minute, the familiar battery and lightning bolt symbol appeared.

He attempted to power the device on, hoping he could operate it while it received the charge. Nothing.

He slammed the blocky monstrosity to the counter and headed back to the pile of mail scattered on the floor. "Well, let's see how bad this is," he mumbled as he scooped the mess into his arms and moved to the couch, placing the heap on the coffee table in front of him.

First order of business was locating the response to his request for essential status. The thought reignited his anger at what had happened earlier that day when he'd visited Stinger Machinery. His first call would be to Agent Woods, then his attorney. What the BHR was doing surely violated his constitutional rights as a business owner and citizen of the United States. Then he recalled how his lawyer had acted when he'd called him months ago, the memory stoking his embers of anger into a fire.

"Lawyers will inherit the first ring of hell," he said, repeating his father's words. How he wished his dad was here to offer his guidance. He had nowhere to turn; the government controlled his life.

His eyes went blurry as tears rolled down his cheeks. Embarrassed, he slammed his eyes shut to stem the flow and thought about what Lisa had said. *We will take it back!*

Reality picked at his mind, threatening to tear free the scab of denial. He allowed the thought to enter and spoke the words to an empty house: "My family may be right."

He shook away the thought and started sorting through the mess on the table. As he'd noticed before, every single envelope had already been opened. And the reason quickly became clear. The contents of each had been removed and haphazardly reinserted into their original envelopes. He conjured up an image of a room stuffed with bespectacled bureaucrats, desks piled high with paperwork, inspecting every piece of mail.

The image faltered when he uncovered a bright pink envelope, return addressed to the BHR. He pulled the contents free and unfolded the letter. Two thin plastic cards fell free.

Setting the letter aside, he picked the cards up. One had his photo and one Lisa's. They were the same ones used on their drivers' licenses. Then his eyes drifted to the bold, red banner above the pictures: "Essential Person: Limited."

"Limited? What the hell does that mean?"

Remembering the letter, he snatched it from the table and read the words that caused his body to shudder:

"The Bureau of Harm Reduction has granted you essential person status, with limitations. You are permitted unrestricted movement on your property. Furthermore, you may attend medical appointments and obtain essential supplies such as food or maintenance items for your owner-occupied residence during normal business hours. If your employer receives essential business status, you may report to that employer's place of business only.

"Social visitations, to include family, must be requested via the Form 85NEV-Nonessential Visitation. Send the completed Form 85NEV to the Bureau of Civic Responsibility, not the Bureau of Harm Reduction, which issued this notice. Failure to complete the form in its entirety or failure to forward the form to the proper department will result in your request being denied.

"You have also been granted e-commerce privileges, limited to essential supplies using Omni-Online. Enter the nineteen-digit number found at the bottom of your essential person pass. Do not share this number with others outside of your resident dwelling.

"Social media access has been denied, as has general internet access. If you would like to appeal our ruling, submit a Form 85SA-Social Access to the Bureau of Civic Responsibility.

"In accordance with President Eden's declaration of Martial Law, and for your safety, we require your government-issued phone to be in your possession at all times, including while in your resident dwelling.

"Thank you for your patience during this troublesome time. Your safety is our primary concern. Sincerely, the Bureau of Harm Reduction."

As the Draconian edicts sank in, Jack felt lightheaded. A feeling of powerlessness swept through him. Eden was relegating them to serfdom, and Jack couldn't do anything about it.

His new gov-issued phone emitted a screeching noise, akin to a bird of prey, that startled him. He bolted to the kitchen and grabbed the brick-like device from the counter. True to the letter, one of his contacts was calling him.

He stifled his anger and pressed the answer button. "Agent Woods, how *gracious* of you to return my calls."

A smiling voice said, "*Mister* Stinger, we have much to discuss."

CHAPTER 28

MOUNT WEATHER

Chief of Staff Roberts rested his head in his hands as the news anchor's voice blared from the monitor in Mount Weather's main conference room, describing the massacres in painfully accurate detail. The talking head appeared nearly giddy, as if reporting on a monetary aid package for the poverty-ravaged children of Burundi.

But he wasn't. He was reporting on five separate attacks on grocery stores across the country. The death toll from the attacks rose with each passing second as drone footage broadcast the gruesome scenes from every location. *We should have made cable news non-essential,* he mused. Then he quickly jotted a note.

Roberts had planned a simple morning of reviewing the encrypted file forwarded to him by Agent Cummings. Instead, he was trying to develop Eden's response to the morning's events. Or, more accurately, the administration's response delivered by Genus.

His calls to Rosos, to determine why he'd ignored Roberts' original plan, had gone unanswered. So he sat, head throbbing, running through workable solutions for two issues his keeper had created.

As he pondered the administration's response to the terrorist attacks, he realized they could exploit the situation to stifle

Congress's demands to speak to Eden. But completely silencing those voices called for another, more forceful action. An action now unfolding two hundred seventy miles away, as the crow flies. He expected an update by early evening on its outcome.

The longer-term, more pressing issue was Eden's physical and mental condition. Rosos' medical team had gone a tad heavy on the amphetamine Vyvanse in the President's last treatment. The concoction, or medicinal stew, as Roberts referred to it, had been extremely effective. Eden had shown signs of his former self. Experiencing far fewer cognitive *episodes* and a mental acuity comparable to ten years ago, he appeared to be, once again, holding the reins of leadership.

Why the medical team had altered the formula remained a mystery. And Rosos' sharp rebuke when Roberts questioned the logic told him that he'd be left to speculate on their motive.

Regardless, with only a handful of people aware of Eden's near-catatonic state, Roberts was now in charge. Genus wasn't briefed on, nor did she appear concerned with, Eden's absence. As long as she received her talking points and a clear view of the teleprompter, she was happy. Roberts suspected she'd be quite pleased if Eden vanished. She was eager to move into the role of Commander-in-Chief and surely prayed the man would quickly exit the office. By wheelchair or casket didn't matter to her, as long as he was gone.

As he reviewed the files forwarded by Agents Woods and Cummings, furiously scribbling notes on key details, his personal phone buzzed. His eyes snapped to the display. Rosos was calling.

"Hello, sir. Thank you for making time for me today." The echo on the line caused Roberts to pause. "Sir, am I on speaker?"

"You are. Do you have a problem, Mister Roberts?" Rosos answered. His thick foreign accent, coupled with the echo, made him nearly impossible to understand.

Roberts' gut tightened. Something was wrong. His keeper was extremely prudent and would never broadcast their conversation for anyone to overhear.

He found his backbone and responded, "In fact, I do. Our conversations comprise sensitive, highly classified information. You, sir, have schooled me repeatedly on the necessity of discretion."

"Mister Roberts, in my country, we have a saying: *A dolgok változnak.* Do you know this saying? Of course you do not. It means *things are changing.*"

Rivulets of sweat traced the curve of Roberts' spine as his posture stiffened. "Change is good, sir. What can I expect from this change you speak of?"

Sarcastic laughter preceded Rosos' mocking voice. "*This change I speak of* is of no concern to you. And pray it never is." His keeper paused, allowing his meaning to sink in. "I have added a member to our team. You will continue to report directly to me, with a dotted line to Mister Zhang Bu."

Roberts threw a shiver. Zhang Bu headed the intelligence apparatus for the Chinese Communist Party. He suddenly felt as if he were underwater, unable to breathe or move, his world tossed sideways. His chest tightened as he forced words from his mouth. "A pleasure to meet—"

"Shut up," Rosos interrupted. "What is this pressing matter you wish to speak of?"

Roberts flushed with anger. He deserved respect, even from this man. He'd been loyal to a fault and expected to be rewarded for it. Tamping his ire, he pushed forward. "Sir, why did you attack five locations when I asked for only one? Countless innocent people have been injured, with dozens killed. Our goal was to instill fear, not murder them."

Rosos remained silent for a long moment before answering. "It seems you have forgotten your place. You are not at liberty to question my tactics. You simply benefit from them. Fear is powerful. However, the catalyst must be sufficient in order to achieve the appropriate level. In this case, we seek the submission of millions who enjoy many freedoms. Freedoms which oppose our goals and must be controlled."

"Sir, I understand the power of fear. But..."

"But nothing!" Rosos yelled. "You now have your fearful subjects. Act on the opportunity, or I'll replace you with someone that will. Start by *saving* them from the boogieman hiding in the corners of their psyche. If you cannot identify what that looks like, it starts with feeding them. Grant some the liberty to work and move about freely while keeping others isolated. Increase the military's presence in the streets. Cut off their flow of information. Our strategy hasn't changed, Mister Roberts. I will not apologize if your vision of our strategy doesn't match the tactics we use. Now, stop wasting time on needless cross-bureau investigations and execute our strategy immediately."

Roberts went ice-cold at the mention of cross-bureau investigations. The revelation that he was not Rosos' singular point of contact unleashed a crippling wave of anxiety. He stumbled to reply, to regain some control. It was useless. "Yes, s-sir," he stuttered, "I'll move forward as planned. Good day."

He waited for Rosos' reply, but the line was silent. Checking the phone's display, he found the call had already ended.

His head went light on his shoulders, and his world tilted hard to the right. He slammed his eyes shut, willing himself to remain conscious. "Stop it!" he screamed. "Get control of yourself. You're still the most powerful man in the country!"

His self-adoration clearing away the fog, he opened his eyes and found the room had stabilized. With a nod, he moved to his laptop and typed out a message: "Vice President Genus, you will address the nation this evening."

CHAPTER 29

JACK STINGER'S HOME

"Agent Woods, I'll take this moment to inform you that you're full of shit!" Jack was talking before his mind could stop him. "I will not allow you, or your goons, to co-manage Stinger Machinery. Those idiots your organization had running my machines are unemployable! One of them was on his way to destroying a twenty-five-thousand-dollar CNC machine. Your proposal is unacceptable."

"*Mister* Stinger," Agent Woods started, "thank you for reminding me about the incident at your business. I'm sorry, our *partnership* business. You're aware that Stinger Machinery is only a functioning entity by the grace of your government, are you not? Without our help, in the form of a very generous loan, Stinger Machinery would have long ago gone bankrupt." She paused, reveling in her power. "Now, with that loan comes certain stipulations."

"What are you talking about?" Jack interrupted.

"*Mister* Stinger, that's no way to speak to your business partner. Please remain silent until I finish speaking. The terms of your loan are clear. The government doesn't loan money to criminals. Especially violent criminals guilty of assault and felony hit and run. It also retains the right to rescind the funds and demand full and immediate repayment of the loan's outstanding principal."

"Hey, I found strangers operating my business, a business I'm forbidden to visit because of this ridiculous lockdown. It was tantamount to finding strangers in my home, and I acted to defend my property."

"Once again," Woods interrupted. "The BHR inserted a team to ensure our joint venture remained operational. By doing so, we kept your loan from falling into default and allowed people to work during this troublesome time. All while keeping you safe. You should be thanking me and your government for our kindness. Show some gratitude, *Mister* Stinger."

"Thanking the government?" Jack shouted. "You're the reason the situation exists. The government is crushing people, ruining lives, and you think you deserve our thanks. Are you kidding me?"

"Indeed we do!" Woods matched Jack's intensity. "You'd all be lost without us. We are the fabric holding society together. The sooner you accept that truth, the sooner life gets back to normal. May I suggest you try supporting our efforts instead of resisting them? Men of your ilk necessitated people like me!"

Stunned by her statement, Jack raced through his options. The government held the power and with it control. His uncle's words—*play the game*—once again rang in his mind. He just needed to make it to the midterms with his business intact. November was just a few months away, and they'd regain balance. And turn it around.

Forcing the words from his mouth, he said, "I suppose you're right. Where would we be without you? I believe we'd be lost." The words were bitter in his mouth.

"That's better, *Mister* Stinger. Now, you'll be receiving a fine for the hit and run. It covers the cost of repairs to the damaged vehicles but allows you to avoid criminal charges."

Biting down on his rage, he simply complied. He had no choice. He'd become a serf to the government machine.

***

He dialed UW's landline the instant his call with Agent Woods ended. His chest tightened when he received the recorded message that the number had been disconnected. Scrolling through the list of contacts loaded into his gov-issued phone, he found his uncle's cell number. Dialing it, he prayed the man had received his new phone and recovered from his anger with Jack.

It surprised him when the call was answered by Lisa on the first ring. "I can't talk. UW is going to the *grocery* store. He needs to have his phone with him. He's leaving now. He'll be at *our* store in twenty. Give my pass to him, and don't bring my government phone. Love you, bye."

Lisa was gone before he could get a word in. But he understood her message. He hoofed it to the door. He was going shopping.

CHAPTER 30

FLEMING'S GROCERY STORE

UW waited in the parking lot, keeping a sharp eye on the National Guard squad blocking the store's entrance with three Humvees. When Jack's Yukon pulled into view, he flashed his headlights once to get his nephew's attention.

The Yukon sped up, then slowed to a crawl as it approached before abruptly pulling into a parking space three away from UW. The youngest of the Stinger clan glanced at his uncle and slowly exited his vehicle, prompting Willis to follow suit.

Jack watched his uncle as he approached, squinting against the early evening sun. Using sign language, he told him it was good to see him.

UW smiled. Whether or not Jack believed what was happening, he was suspicious enough to communicate in silence. "Good to see you too," he replied using sign. "I think we may have a problem. The store appears closed. Those guardsmen haven't moved, and not a single person has tried to get past them."

Jack's eyebrows raised at the news. He took in the nearly full parking lot and noticed people just sitting in their cars, glancing nervously between them and the store's entrance.

UW tapped Jack on the shoulder to get his attention. "I think I know what's happening. Did you hear the news?"

Jack shook his head and fixed his uncle in a quizzical stare. "The radio is just static on some stations and PSAs on others. I didn't watch the news before I left. What's up?"

His uncle gave a somber nod. "Five grocery stores were bombed this morning. Last update has seventy dead and hundreds injured. They struck at the height of the morning shopping rush. My guess? Every grocery store in the country is closed. You know, for our safety during these troublesome times."

Jack chuckled. "Troublesome times. The new battle cry for bureaucratic overreach." He paused before asking, "What do you make of the government-issued phones? And the other bullshit they're pulling?"

Willis' features went hard as he locked Jack in a withering stare. "You know what I make of it?" his hands moving rapidly as he signed his response. "This is only the beginning. And you need to get onboard. The midterms will change nothing. Don't you see it? There's already talk of holding elections by mail-in ballot only. You know how that'll end."

Jack could see the anger in his uncle's response. His position hadn't changed, and nothing Jack could say would alter that. As he thought through his response, doubt in his own beliefs began picking at his mind. "Who told you about their plans for the elections?"

UW avoided the question. "Let's take a walk," he said while pushing his chin at the Guardsmen.

Jack didn't object or push UW to answer his question. He simply followed his uncle's lead and headed towards the store's entrance. As they walked, the frightened faces of hundreds of people watched them, some exiting their safe spaces and taking positions leaning against their cars.

An odd feeling overcame Jack as they neared the National Guard's position. He felt defiant, as if he was pushing back against the government machine. The realization rattled him. *When did trying to buy groceries become heroic?*

UW snapped into the role of USMC colonel the instant a Guardsman moved to intercept them. "Stand down, soldier. I'm Colonel Willis Stinger, USMC, retired. This parking lot is full of *civilians* that need food. We'll be entering this store, with or without your permission. Are you prepared to pull the trigger on innocents?"

The young soldier, at first unsure how to respond, suddenly shouldered his weapon. "Sir, as a soldier, you'll understand I'm acting on orders. Return to your vehicle and leave the area."

Willis continued walking towards the Guardsman as Jack slammed to a stop. "Son, find your commanding officer before I do something you'll regret later in life, probably when you're trying to have children." His uncle's tone left no doubt that he'd already determined what he would do to the soldier and how he would do it.

Jack watched in amazement as the soldier lowered his weapon and called out for someone named Sergeant Segar. UW stopped his menacing advance only after the soldier acted on his recommendation.

Willis turned towards Jack and, using sign language, told him to remain calm and not to say a word, no matter what happened. It confused him, but he followed his uncle's directions.

A moment later, a beefy man sporting three stripes on his sleeve stood shoulder to shoulder with the young Guardsman.

"What's the issue, Gorman?" the sergeant barked.

"Segar?" Willis questioned. "Related to Major Alex Segar?"

"Who's asking?" Segar replied suspiciously.

"Colonel Willis Stinger, USMC, retired. And I suppose it's not important who you're related to. What is important is helping hungry people get food. Why isn't that happening, Sergeant?"

"Orders, sir. No entry until I receive the all-clear. It's for their safety."

"I don't give a flying rat's ass about your orders. And if one more person tells me it's for my safety, I will certainly kick their ass."

Segar's posture stiffened as he took a half step towards UW. "Is that a threat? I don't take kindly to threats to my men. That includes threats from retired Marine colonels. Now, state your business."

"I see from your response you are, in fact, related to Major Segar. You display the same blind obedience to your commander as he did. And so we're clear, I don't take kindly to having an M4 pointed at my chest, so we're even." He paused, glancing at the tense faces of the Guardsmen watching the exchange.

"Sergeant, walk with me," UW said. "I'll explain what 'duty to disobey' means as defined by the UCMJ (Uniform Code of Military Justice)."

UW didn't wait for Segar's response. He turned and handed Jack his gov-issued cell. Then, using sign language, he said, "Hold this while I talk to the sergeant. If any soldiers try to talk to you, reply with sign, or write a note telling them you're deaf." His devious grin told Jack he was enjoying himself.

As an uneasy Sergeant Segar walked down the sidewalk with UW, Jack was left standing in silence with seven twitchy Guardsmen. It only took a few seconds before Gorman, the soldier who'd originally confronted them, spoke.

"What's the story with the colonel? He doesn't seem to know he's retired. Acting like an ass-hat if you ask me."

Jack almost responded but stopped himself. Instead, feigning confusion, he pointed to his ears while shaking his head.

With a smirk, Gorman turned away and rejoined his squad, laughing at an unheard joke. *He was baiting me,* Jack thought as he watched the Guardsman huddle with his comrades. *What would he have done if I slipped?* The thought sent a chill down his spine.

These weren't the soldiers he'd been raised to respect. They were the local level enforcement arm of Eden's administration. *Freshly vetted Gestapo.*

Suddenly uneasy, Jack took a few steps back, trying to put some distance between him and the soldiers. He risked a glance in the direction his uncle had walked with Sergeant Segar. He felt some relief when he found the men walking in his direction.

The feeling was fleeting as he got a read on UW. His uncle's face was a mask of anger. Perhaps fury was a better description. As he made eye contact with Jack, his hands began signing, "This jackass is brainwashed. Head to your SUV. I'll meet you in a second."

"They're all brainwashed. And I'll wait with you," Jack replied.

"What's with the mute? Kinda creepy the way you two talk with your hands. Is he retarded?"

Segar was staring into Willis' rage-filled eyes before he realized the old Marine had moved into his path. "What was that, Sergeant?" he asked in a growling whisper.

Jack was moving to intervene as Segar stuttered through a dozen words, unable to string a sentence together. He quickened his pace as his uncle's posture went stiff and his hands balled into fists.

Jack glanced over his shoulder to check on Segar's squad. He found they had moved to a position on the far side of the closest Humvee, blocking their view of the confrontation between UW and Segar. He quickly noticed their defensive posture as two men holding strange blocky weapons he'd never seen moved forward as the remaining soldiers readied their battle rifles.

Jack followed the Guardsmen's stare as an angry voice reached him. Spinning hard to his right, he saw a crowd of people gathered at the edge of the parking lot, twenty feet away. A mountain of a man fronted what was rapidly becoming an angry mob, and Jack quickly determined the voice belonged to him.

"Who do you people think you are? You can't do this to us. My family needs food!" the man screamed.

Jack looked in his uncle's direction and found UW and Segar silently staring wide-eyed at the mob. He locked eyes with his uncle and nodded. They were at a full run a second later.

"Follow me to my house," UW yelled while keeping pace with the younger Stinger.

Jack's reply was cut off as gunfire rang out behind them.

CHAPTER 31

PETER MATHEWS' HOME

Mathews was watching the 85 Plumbing truck from his second-story bedroom window. It hadn't moved in weeks, and he'd seen no one get in or out of it. He'd decided to find out what was going on.

"Yep, this is perfect," he said while grabbing the security camera from its case. He quickly clamped its base to the windowsill, linked it to a one terabyte external hard drive, and configured it to record continuously.

As he positioned the camera, two things happened: Willis' truck, followed by an oversized SUV, barreled down the street and quickly pulled into UW's driveway. As the SUV disappeared into his friend's garage, he saw Thatcher walking towards his home.

"What the hell do you want? I swear I will end you if you pull any bullshit with me." He'd no sooner finished his rant than he heard a knock on his door. He considered ignoring it, but another, more forceful knock followed. "Even your knock sounds wussy. God, I hate this kid!"

He powered up the camera, waited until the indicator light flashed, covered the red blinking light with electrical tape, then rumbled downstairs.

Mathews reached the door as Thatcher began knocking, harder, more frantic than before. He yanked the heavy oak door open and locked Thatcher in a challenging glare. The younger man took a step back, appearing to contemplate jumping from the porch and running screaming back to his wife and stinky baby. But he recovered quickly, features hardening in grim determination.

"What do you want, Thatcher?" Mathews noticed the essential person pass hanging from a lanyard dangling from his gaunt neck. "Why are you wearing that thing? You're literally fifty steps from your front door."

"Hello, Officer Mathews, sorry to bother you. I need food to feed my infant child. We've been unable to leave our resident dwelling to go shopping for several weeks, and we've run out... we have nothing to eat. To answer your question, we're supposed to wear them at all times, even while in our resident dwelling."

Mathews stood, dumbfounded by Thatcher's audacity and struggling against his first instinct to snap his neighbor's neck. "You're joking; this is a joke, right? I mean... really, you're asking *me* for food?"

Mathews' gaze dropped to Thatcher's essential person badge. For the first time, he noticed it was a different color than his. Focusing on the boldface font, he caught the words: "Unrestricted—No Limitations."

"How d'you get that?" he asked, nodding at the man's badge.

"Um, we all got them. You just asked me about it, so I'm confused by your question."

"No, numbnuts. Unrestricted No Limitation status."

"Oh," Thatcher said, holding his badge up to inspect it. "I don't know, we just received them, and that's our assigned status."

As he dropped his badge back to his chest, Mathews noticed the iPhone in Thatcher's shirt pocket. Its camera faced out. At the same instant, a glint of light flashed from the 85 Plumbing van's side.

Confused, he focused on the area where he thought the light came from when it happened again. A twinkle of light from below the number "8" halfway up the van's side body, immediately behind the cab.

He looked over his shoulder, trying to determine what someone parked in front of his house at that exact moment could see. Relieved by the area's relative emptiness, he turned to face Thatcher.

"Where's your gov-issued phone, Thatcher?" he said as he crossed the threshold onto the porch, shutting the door behind him. "And why are you recording me?"

Thatcher's eyes went wide as Mathews halved the distance between them. Taking a reflexive step back, he pulled his hands up in a blocking motion, anticipating another assault. "We didn't get ours yet. We'll start using them as soon as we get them. I promise."

Mathews nodded in understanding. "Oh, you didn't get them? My contacts tell me no one, not a single person, knew the government's plan to distribute phones. I sure as hell didn't. Tell me something, Thatcher. If you haven't left your house, how did you know about the phones? You've also used the *resident dwelling* buzzword and received your badges. So, I'm calling bullshit. Where's your government phone?"

As Thatcher sputtered through random words, trying to form a sentence, Mathews cut him off. "Thatcher, do you understand that those people, the government's goons that sent you to spy on me, aren't your friends? They couldn't care less about you or your family. What'd they offer you, food, a little *extra* freedom, or something more enticing? My guess is you were all too eager to help them and probably volunteered. Proud to serve your country by spying on people you hate."

Thatcher's eyes narrowed as he smirked. "You can't touch me, not this time. And I'm proud of what I've done. I did it because people like you caused the problems we face today. Running around with your guns, talking about liberty while you oppress entire communities. The government should lock you away, all of you."

He glanced over his shoulder at the van, then back to Mathews. "Now, I need food and we know you have some. So, strut yourself into your kitchen, figure out what you can live without, and bring it to me. Or I'll send my *friends* in to take it."

Mathews stepped in Thatcher's direction, eliciting a yelp from the bone-thin man. "You have thirty seconds to remove your worthless hide from my property. Oh, and Thatcher, your *infant child* smells like poop. Give it a bath, for God's sake!"

He took another menacing step toward his neighbor, causing Thatcher to turn quickly and slither off his porch. As he scurried across his lawn, Mathews noticed the large block-shaped bulge in the back pocket of Thatcher's filthy skinny jeans.

"I'll be sure to tell your keepers you're a terrible liar!" he barked as Thatcher quickened his pace.

Watching until his neighbor disappeared into his home, he turned his focus on the ever-present van. He resisted the urge to confront its occupants, hidden within, opting instead for a friendly wave. "Your time is coming," he growled through clenched teeth.

CHAPTER 32

WILLIS STINGER'S HOME

Jack held his wife in a tight embrace, breathing in the scent of her freshly washed hair. For a fleeting moment, he felt safe again, normal. She attempted to end the moment, but he increased his grip in response, willing the moment to last a little longer.

"Okay, Jack. Time to let go. I need to dry my hair," she squeaked while wrenching herself from his arms.

"Do you know what I love most about you?" Jack said. "You're so, what's the word, caring. That's it, caring. Do you understand that we're broke, our life savings has been destroyed? That armed soldiers were firing on people because a food riot was breaking out, in *America*. In our *country*! The government seized control of our business, and our ability to move freely has been taken away. Those things aren't supposed to happen!"

Lisa stomped away while rolling her eyes and shaking her head. "I appreciate how you must be feeling after what happened at the store. But, at the end of the day, they didn't shoot at you, Jack. You don't know if they were actually shooting *at* people or firing warning shots into the air. We don't know because you and your uncle ran away. We're never running away again. And I already told you, we're going to take everything back, everything!

Stop being so dramatic. We can't afford drama. Show some resolve, Jack. We need a plan. So find UW and get to work."

"Such a sweet, sweet lady."

"What was that, Jack?"

Jack was startled. He'd thought he was whispering. "Uh, nothing, just wondering out loud where UW's hiding. That's twice that you said *we're going to take it back*. What's that mean, exactly? How are you planning to do that?"

Lisa poked her head around the corner, a disbelieving look crossing her features. "Willis is in the garage where you left him five minutes ago. Talk to him; he'll explain it."

"Oh yeah, I must have forgotten. You know, from being lost in my wife's loving embrace."

Lisa rolled her eyes again and flipped on the blow-dryer, officially ending the conversation.

"She's a spitfire." His uncle's voice forced a startled jump from him. "Settle down, Jack. When'd you get so twitchy?"

UW's smile faded as he gazed into Jack's eyes. His nephew was tough, always had been. But they hadn't been in a drunken barroom brawl this afternoon.

"Sorry, Jack. I was out of line."

"No reason to apologize. I *am* acting twitchy. I just can't believe… can't wrap my head around what happened today. Or any of this, for that matter. What's happening to our country, UW?"

Willis shushed Jack while shaking his head and holding up his gov-issued cell. "Use sign language only," he signed as he increased the volume of the radio sitting on his coffee table, bringing its static-filled speaker to near deafening levels.

Jack gave UW a curious stare but realized he wasn't questioning the man's sanity as he had a couple of weeks ago. His uncle remained close to his military family; men and women with access to information the average person could only imagine existed. Jack knew he had to accept that reality and the possibility that his country, his government, was plotting against its citizens.

UW read Jack's expression and smiled. "I've seen that look before," he signed while nodding at Jack. "Truth and understanding can be bitter pills. But they must be swallowed."

His uncle was interrupted by a strange chirping sound emitted from his shirt pocket. Jack watched as UW retrieved a sleek black object from his pocket, unfolded what appeared to be an antenna from its side, and focused all of his attention on the object.

After a few seconds, Jack realized his uncle held a phone, the likes of which he'd never seen. His curiosity was piqued as the man furiously pressed unseen keys, typing a message Jack was determined to know more about.

Willis finished and caught his nephews eye's as he placed the phone back in his pocket. "It's a sat-phone," he signed. "That was a text from Peter. It seems our government has enlisted the plebeians. I'll explain later, but right now…."

The screeching from Jack's phone cut UW off. Startled by the noise, Jack flinched, then pulled the unsightly gov-phone from his pocket. His breath caught as he read the message displayed on its screen: "The Bureau of Harm Reduction has not authorized your current location. Essential person privileges for Jack Stinger are limited. Return to your resident dwelling immediately. Failure to do so will result in restrictions being placed on your movements. Thank you for your patience during these troublesome times."

Stunned to silence, he handed the phone to his uncle, who, after reading the message, locked Jack in a hard stare. "Get home," he said, "and I've got something for you."

UW raced to the garage with Jack in tow. He reached into his truck, retrieved a box, and shoved it into his nephew's hand. Jack glanced at the box and realized they had reached a tipping point. His focus shifted between the box and his uncle, finally locking on the box as he read the label: "IsatPhone 2."

"Son of a bitch, I knew they'd do it!" UW signed. "Get moving, Jack. I'll let Lisa know what's happening. Charge its battery, then text me. We have a lot to talk about."

CHAPTER 33

JACK STINGER'S HOME

Jack checked his watch as the garage door closed. "You, Jack Stinger, just broke the land speed record. Hey, BHR, if you're listening, I'm home like a good little sheep." He wanted to laugh at his wit, but the day's chaos wouldn't allow it. He rested his head on the seat's plush leather and blew air through puffed cheeks, wondering if the Bureau of Harm Reduction really was listening. *Things will never be the same.* The thought sent dozens of emotions to war in his mind. Shaking them away, he exited the cab with his new satellite phone in hand.

Jack threw a shiver as he entered his home. The recent cold snap made it feel more like early fall than mid-spring, enhancing the feeling of dread slowly consuming him. He tossed the phone on the kitchen counter and walked to the thermostat. "Well, dumbass, maybe you should've turned it on!" he said as he selected the heat function on the digital thermostat.

He stood motionless, hating how quiet his home was without Lisa, hating what his world was becoming. The thump of his mailbox cover slamming shut drew his attention.

Hurrying back to the kitchen, he unboxed the sat-phone, quickly located the charging cord, and plugged it in. He waited for the charging indicator to blink, set it down, and headed to retrieve his mail.

The now-familiar plastic bag containing opened and inspected mail hit the coffee table with a heavy slap. Jack breathed deep before plowing forward, preparing himself to find dozens of past-due notices mixed in with whatever new edicts the government had decided to impose upon the people.

The thought had no sooner formed than he noticed an envelope from the Bureau of Civic Responsibility. Jack's stomach lurched. *Please, God, don't let them take anything else from me.*

Hands shaking, he retrieved the envelope and removed the letter. Relieved at first, Jack's anger quickly took hold as he read: "Congratulations. The Bureau of Civic Responsibility has created a new account in your name with the online retailer, Omni-Online. To avoid confusion, your existing account was closed.

"Your government deposited fifteen hundred dollars to your Omni-Online account to help you purchase essential products during these troublesome times. A list of items you're authorized to acquire is located in your account profile.

"Using Omni-Online for your purchases will ease the strain placed on essential retailers across the country and allow you to remain safe while securing your essential items.

"If you find the authorized products inadequate, submit the Form 85EER-Essentials Expansion Request to the Bureau of Civic Responsibility. We will review each request for expansion as time permits.

"We thank you for your patience and understanding as we work to keep you safe during these troublesome times."

The message became clear. Total control. Jack's anger surged. He crumpled the letter and threw it across the living room. He gazed at the pile of open mail and swept it from the table. His mind was on fire as his eyes blurred with tears.

"How did we let this happen?" he screamed as he bolted to his feet. "You work for *us*." His voice shook with emotion as he paced back and forth, feeling the walls close in with each step.

As Jack spun to traverse his living room a tenth time, an unfamiliar chirping reached him from the kitchen. His confusion cleared as he remembered the sat-phone charging on the countertop. He made a beeline to the kitchen to retrieve the phone. Expecting to find a welcome message from the phone's manufacturer, it surprised him when a text message notification appeared on the phone's display.

He tapped the message icon and found a simple message: "News conference happening now."

CHAPTER 34

RAVEN ROCK MOUNTAIN MILITARY COMPLEX

With less than thirty seconds until her address to the nation, Vice President Genus reviewed her prepared comments for the first time. Roberts watched via video from Mount Weather as her eyes told the story of a school child unprepared for the pop quiz she was just handed.

"Where's the teleprompter?" she screamed to someone off-camera, panic shrilling her voice.

Roberts watched as Genus' eyes searched the surrounding area, desperate to find the machine that would feed her the information she'd been too lazy to review over the last four hours.

"Vice President Genus, you have fifteen seconds. Pull yourself together. America needs to see strong leadership. Right now, you're displaying anything but strength."

"Why isn't Eden delivering this address?" she countered.

"For the love of God!" Roberts barked. "Did you review any of the prepared remarks? The President has fallen ill. He's being cared for by a small army of medical professionals. You're running the *show*, so to speak."

Roberts nearly burst into laughter as the color drained from her face. "You're on, *Madam* Vice President," he said with a smirk.

After stuttering through ten seconds of incoherent babble, Genus pulled a calming breath and launched into her address to the nation.

"Many of you are probably wondering why President Eden isn't delivering this news. I'm saddened to tell you that our dear leader has fallen ill. His medical team is hard at work trying to identify the cause of his condition, and we will update you as soon as we have information. But rest assured, your government is still functioning. And we're working tirelessly to keep all of you safe during these troublesome times."

"Stop ad-libbing," Roberts hissed into his microphone, causing Genus to flinch and press a hand to her ear. "Read the remarks as written!"

Genus paused, then restarted her address after Roberts' voice faded from her earpiece. "With that said, I want to address the horrible events from this morning. If you aren't aware, five separate bombings claimed dozens of innocent lives and injured countless others across our great nation. Our intelligence community has confirmed that the domestic terrorists that have plunged our country into this crisis are responsible."

Genus shuffled through the papers laid out on the table in front of her, appearing to have lost her place after Roberts' interruption. With a jerk of her head, as if remembering she was on live television, she plowed forward. "Later in the day, a food riot broke out at a store in the great state of O-hi-o." Nervous cackling laughter followed the bizarre pronunciation before she jolted herself back into the role of concerned politician.

"This event required our National Guard to fire on the rioters using rubber bullets. No serious injuries were reported, but the situation could have ended in yet another tragedy."

Genus' breath hitched as she scanned the next line. She looked into the camera, then back at her papers. "Um, due to the unavoidable and persistent challenges to the essential products supply chain, coupled with the horrific events we witnessed earlier today... Your government will take the reins of our national food distribution. You should have, by now, received a letter from the Bureau of Civic Responsibility informing you that, um, a new Omni-Online account has been created in your name. Additionally, your government has deposited fifteen hundred dollars to help you safely purchase essential products. If you are unable or unwilling to use your new account, the Bureau of Harm Reduction, working in conjunction with the Bureau of Civic Responsibility, will begin meal delivery services next week."

"Speak up, you twit, you're practically whispering. Try projecting some strength," Roberts growled.

Genus, flushed with anger, held the camera in a contemptuous glare meant for Roberts.

"Congratulation, *Madam* Vice President, the entire population of the United States now thinks you're giving them a dirty look. Snap out of it, and wrap up this cluster of a news conference. NOW!"

In a near snarl, Genus said, "Food will be delivered by sector and on assigned days. We will provide more information soon."

Taking a deep breath, she again studied her prepared remarks before continuing. "To add to the tragic and violent day, we lost our beloved Senator Rodman to the assassins' bullet. Due to this, and for the safety of the public and our brave frontline workers, the Bureau of Harm Reduction will be taking *temporary* control of civilian firearms. Firearms will be returned after the threat to our safety is neutralized. To accomplish this overwhelming and potentially violent, but extremely necessary, task, we call on our citizen soldiers to help identify friends, family, and neighbors who own or have access to firearms."

Genus stopped speaking and stared blankly into the camera.

"You're not finished!" Roberts yelled.

The Vice President flinched, then flashed a smile akin to a lunatic before continuing the national address. "Our intelligence community has determined that the terrorists may be using the country's media outlets to convey coded messages. These messages aid the terrorists in organizing their despicable activities. Therefore, we are suspending the media's broadcast privileges until we have fully vetted them and determine they can be trusted. Your government will allow access to a library of approved movies for your viewing enjoyment. Directions for accessing this library will be mailed to your resident dwelling."

"Very good. Now, wrap it up," Roberts commanded.

Genus nodded. "I understand we are all eager to get back to normal, to visit friends and loved ones, and to leave our homes without fear. And I promise you that our administration is working hard to make that happen. Until then, we ask that you remain patient during these troublesome times. From my family to yours, we're in this together. Stay strong, America."

CHAPTER 35

JACK STINGER'S HOME

Jack shut off the television as the vice president stared into the camera like a deer caught in headlights. His anger peaked as he threw the remote against the wall, shattering it into a dozen shards of jagged plastic.

"You must be out of your mind!" His voice echoed through his empty house, reminding him he was still alone.

He shot to his feet as the sat-phone chirped with a newly received message. "Citizen soldiers! They just painted targets on our backs!"

Jack began typing a response when what sounded like a small army of vehicles rumbling down his street grabbed his attention. He shoved the phone into his back pocket and headed towards the window. The sight greeting him when he pulled back the drapes sent ice through his veins.

A line of half a dozen 85 Plumbing vans sat idling in front of his house. As he watched, all but one pulled to strategic locations along his street, two of them blocking the entrances at either end.

"What the actual hell is happening?" His question was answered as a group of men dressed in black exited the back of the van parked three homes away and stormed up the driveway of his friend Dale Winters' home.

At that moment, their intent became clear. Dale was a hunter and owned several high-end rifles. As Jack scanned the locations of the other vans, he realized they had all taken up positions in front of the homes of people he knew owned firearms.

Backing away from the window, he yanked the sat-phone free and typed a simple message: "85 Plumbing making move. Hide your guns."

He hit send as he bolted upstairs, searching for a place to hide the presumably illegal phone. Now he understood why UW had insisted Jack bring all but a few of his firearms to be kept at his home. But why would the government ignore his uncle's home as well? UW had to understand that when they moved to disarm the public, he'd be on the list, and they'd find the guns when his home was searched.

Not important now, Jack. His self admonishment focused him on the task at hand. He rushed into his bedroom and tapped the side of the QLine nightstand with the RFID key-fob which released the spring-loaded false-side. He slapped the phone into the compartment next to his Glock 17 and slammed it shut.

He hurried downstairs to the kitchen, tossed the key-fob into the bowl where they kept their keys and loose change, and waited for the knock on his door he knew was coming.

A flash later, a hard knock followed by the repeated ringing of his doorbell caused him to take a deep, calming breath. He knew what had to happen and thought about the quick access gun case resting on his desk upstairs holding his Ruger LCP. He knew after today he'd never see it again.

As he crossed the living room to answer the door, he winced when he remembered the two 1911 safe-queens resting in his nearly empty gun safe in the basement. He'd never fired them and rarely handled them. But he loved them and had paid a small fortune for each; parting with them wouldn't be easy.

Another hard knock was followed by a muffled threat of forced entry.

"Relax!" he bellowed, then realized he wasn't supposed to know who was at his door. "Who the hell are you, and why are you bagging on my door?" he asked before opening the door.

"Mister Stinger, we represent the Bureau of Harm Reduction. We're here to remove any dangerous weapons from your home for temporary safe-keeping at our secured facility. Open the door immediately or we will enter by force."

Any dangerous weapons. Jack scowled as he unlocked the deadbolt. His thoughts were cut short as two BHR operators pushed through, shouldering MP5s, and forced Jack out of their way. Their black tactical clothing was more suited for covert government operations than patrolling suburbia in search of legally owned firearms.

As they swept the area for threats, two more operators barged into his home, with one of them taking a position to block Jack from moving. The other heel-toed through the first floor, yelling "Clear" as he finished searching each room.

"Um, little intense, don't you think?" Jack intoned while biting back his rage and repeating his uncle's words in his mind. *Play the game.* "I suppose you're here for my gun. You'll find it in my office, second floor, first door on the right. I'll be expecting a receipt before you leave."

The BHR operator blocking his path said with a sarcastic grin, "Yeah, sure, a receipt. Coming right up. And we're here for all your guns, not just the LCP. Looking forward to seeing those high-end 1911s."

Jack held a straight face and prayed his expression wasn't betraying his anger and shock at the knowledge the man held regarding his firearms. Specifically, knowing the makes and models. "Oh, that's right; I forgot about them," Jack said while feigning poor memory.

"Oh, you forgot about two, not one, but two Dan Wesson 1911s. What about your long guns, Mister Stinger. Did you *forget* about those as well?"

"Nah, I remembered those. I sold them a while ago. They were just collecting dust." Jack kept his tone even while fighting the urge to throat punch the man. "Where's your name patch? I'd like to know the names of the people illegally seizing my weapons."

"Name's not important; it'll be on your *receipt*. What *is* important is that our records show you have eight guns in your possession. Meaning we need to return to base with eight weapons or I'll have to fill out a ton of paperwork. So, who'd you sell your guns to? Or did you forget that too?"

"Base?" Jack questioned. "Like a military base? Why would you need a *base*? And I don't remember the buyer's information; it was a while ago." Motioning to his head, he added, "Poor memory and all."

The BHR operator flashed a wicked grin and grabbed his shoulder-mounted radio. "Well, boys. Mister Stinger has decided to be difficult. We'll be performing a deep search of his home. Turn it over. We have eight guns to find."

***

Jack walked through his house, picking his way through the mess left behind by the Bureau of Harm Reduction. He'd watched as they rampaged through his home, gleefully trashing every inch. The contents of every dresser drawer, closet, cupboard, and shelf now lay scattered on the floor.

He'd watched nervously as they trashed his bedroom and focused on the nightstand holding the sat-phone. Mercifully, the RFID lock held the hidden side compartment shut as they yanked the front drawer to the floor.

After the first fifteen minutes, Jack understood they weren't searching for his guns. They were enjoying themselves and sending a message. *We're in control, and we can do anything we want.*

Overwhelmed, he took a seat at his dining room table and stared at the destruction. His family had been right. "We're going to take it back, all of it." Repeating his wife's words set a fire in his soul. One that burned hotter with every passing second.

His thoughts of revenge snapped when his gov-issued phone emitted the screech of an incoming call. He didn't need to see the display. He knew who was calling.

"Hello, Agent Woods. To what do I owe the honor of hearing your harmonic tones?"

Taken aback by his calm demeanor, Woods paused for a moment. "*Mister* Stinger, I understand you were less than cooperative this evening. That's not what we want from our business partners. Something we'll need to work on."

"Sure, I'll get right on that. Wouldn't want to upset my partners," Jack answered in the same flat tone with which he'd answered the call.

"I'm confident you will. However, your poor behavior isn't the reason for my call. Our partnership requires you to be present at Stinger Machinery. Although your government possesses superior management skills, it lacks in other areas. We expect to see you at our joint venture tomorrow morning. You'll be granted permission to bring back select staff members to supplement the workers we've provided."

"I'm surprised," Jack interrupted. "With everyone locked in their homes, who needs car parts? No one's driving."

"Oh, that's right," Woods said, "you're unaware of the manufacturing changes we've implemented." The statement caused Jack's teeth to grind. "You're now manufacturing much-needed supplies for your government. We're a very good customer. You'll be briefed when you arrive in the morning."

Play the game. "I'm very excited, Agent Woods. It sounds like an extraordinary opportunity to support my government's efforts." Jack nearly gagged on his words.

"It is, *Mister* Stinger. One you'd be wise to take advantage of."

"I'm a wise man, Agent Woods. Now, if you have nothing further, I should get to work putting my home back together. Your troops were very thorough. It was extraordinary to watch them work."

After a long pause, Woods said, "Well, since you've asked. I have another matter to discuss. Your wife, Lisa, hasn't activated her new phone. Nor did our agents report seeing her. We have information that she was temporarily living in your uncle's resident dwelling but have since confirmed she isn't there. Where has she run off to?"

Panic set in. Jack didn't know why, but his mind screamed at him to lie. "She left me, Agent Woods. The stress was getting to me, and the changes in my personality were too much. Our marriage quickly fell apart. I haven't spoken to her since she moved out of my uncle's. I suppose the only reason I haven't been served with divorce papers is because of the lockdown." He cringed at the insincerity in his voice.

"Well, that's very sad to hear." Woods' voice dripped with cynicism. "I'll make a note to have our agents find her. We can't have an unhappy business partner."

Jack slammed his eyes shut and took a deep breath. "I'd appreciate that, Agent Woods. Thank you. I guess the government really is here to help."

CHAPTER 36

WILLIS STINGER'S HOME

UW grabbed the gov-issued phone from his back pocket. His eyebrows hitched in disbelief when he saw Jack's number displayed. *Why are you texting me on this phone, Jack?* His anger surged at the thought of his nephew being this reckless. He was still furious that the Bureau of Harm Reduction had searched his home, and Jack's thoughtless action put him over the edge.

Confusion set in when he read the message: "Stinger Machinery has rehired you. Report to work by 7 a.m."

He set the gov-phone down and retrieved the sat-phone from his shirt pocket. Typing furiously on the small display, he hit send just as Jack's call came through.

"Jack?" UW answered, worried the BHR had discovered the sat-phone.

"It's me. I should have called before sending the text. You ready to go back to work? Do me a favor and go outside or turn on your radio before you talk."

"What the hell are you talking about?" UW's frustration bubbled through, but he appeased his nephew and turned on his radio.

"I've been granted the ability to work in *my* business. The government is so wonderful," Jack said sarcastically. "I figured you and me in the same building would make it easier to communicate. Do me a favor, check the bottom of any heavy furniture the BHR didn't flip over or manhandle. You'll see what I mean. It's why I'm calling you from outside."

Understanding setting in, Willis paused before answering Jack. "So, what would we be communicating about?"

"I think you know," Jack answered. "Agent Woods asked about Lisa. She hinted that they didn't see her when they searched your house. I don't know what you did, but keep it that way. I told her Lisa left me, but they'll be sniffing around." Jack paused. "How bad was it, the search? They tore my place apart."

"I gave them hell the entire time they were here, but they still inflicted a fair amount of damage. Told them I lost most of my guns in a boating accident. I think the dumb bastards actually believed me. I sacrificed two Hi-Points to appease our overlords. It's why I bought them in the first place. Lisa's safe. I'll explain when I see you at work tomorrow. Anything else?"

"Nope, see you in the morning. Don't be late."

Willis disconnected the call as a smile creased his features. Jack was coming around. Reality was taking hold.

He considered texting his nephew to ask how much Stinger Machinery would pay, maybe bust his chops about being a tightwad. But he glanced up from his phone and took in his surroundings. His home was a wreck. But his heavy wood coffee table remained untouched.

Remembering what Jack said, he walked to the table and got down on his knees to inspect it. It took less than thirty seconds for him to figure out what his nephew meant. A silver dollar-sized disk was attached to the table's underside. *A bug, you sneaky bastards!*

UW pushed himself up and headed for the kitchen. He quickly found what he was searching for. The BHR had emptied his cupboards of every pot and pan he owned. Payback time! A crooked grin curled his lips as he picked up a five-quart stainless steel pot from the floor and filled it with a handful of silverware.

Standing next to the coffee table, he raised the pan over his head then slammed it to the ground. The noise on impact was deafening, but he couldn't stop himself from breaking into muffled hysterics imagining a now-deaf BHR operative rolling around the floor of the 85 Plumbing van parked in front of his home.

"I hope your ears are bleeding," he snarled just above a whisper.

CHAPTER 37

FOURTEEN MONTHS POST INAUGURATION, STINGER MACHINERY

Jack pulled into the parking lot of Stinger Machinery at quarter till seven. The sunrise promised a brilliant day as he gazed at the building that had been in his life since childhood. It felt good to be here.

His mood soured when a Toyota Prius rolled into a parking space in front of him. His eye twitched as he watched the gray-suited BHR Observer exit the tiny electric nightmare. The Observer's smug grin nearly drove Jack to stomp on the accelerator and run him down. He quickly shut his Yukon off to avoid a life sentence for murder, opting instead to plaster on a fake smile and greet him with a wave.

"Hey, good to see you again. Sorry about the incident. No hard feelings?" he said as he exited his SUV and approached the Observer. "I hope you weren't hurt. Just kind of lost my cool when I found people in my business without me."

"*Our* business, Jack. This is now a partnership. It's imperative you accept that this company is now a joint venture."

Jack took a calming breath, but his smile never faltered. "You're correct; I'll work on my attitude towards our partnership.

It'll take some adjusting, but I'll eventually get it right, partner."
He offered his hand, which the Observer ignored.

"You'd better get it *right*, and I suggest you do so quickly.
We must show unity inside that building, make the worker bees
understand who's in charge. Something we've struggled with of
late."

Jack stiffened at the Observer's "worker bees" comment,
bringing an arrogant smile to the man's face.

"Speaking of *worker bees*. Which ones are you bringing back?
I'll need to approve them before they can begin working. I have
the specs for the new products Stinger Machinery is producing.
I'm confident you and your ilk will approve of them."

"I'm eager to hear more," Jack forced through gritted teeth.
"I brought back Randy, Armin, and Willis. But something tells
me you already knew that." The comment slipped past his
cooperative veneer.

Displaying a greasy smile, the Observer slowly nodded,
confirming Jack's assumption.

Jack questioned his ability to maintain his charade as UW's
truck rumbled into the parking lot and pulled into a parking
space.

His uncle hopped out of the truck and moved like the wind
toward him. The intensity of his stare told Jack he was worried
about what was happening between him and the gray suit.

UW had halved the distance when Jack signed to him that
everything was fine. Receiving a nod of understanding, he turned
back to the gray suit. The man was pinching the bridge of his
nose, an expression of disgust clearly visible.

"Another one, Jack? That man, Randy, was incredibly
difficult to interact with. Do you have an arrangement with the

NAD (National Association of the Deaf?) Can't you re-hire someone normal that I can communicate with?"

"Normal?" Jack asked as he locked the Observer in a withering glare. "In an effort to maintain our partnership, I'm going to ignore that comment... once. If you want to communicate with our hearing-impaired *worker bees*, I suggest you learn sign language. I can have Randy teach you the basics."

Recoiling from Jack's sharp tone, the BHR Observer stumbled through his reply. "No, no, I have many important things to accomplish on a condensed timeline. And, of course, I meant no insult to any of the physically impaired members of our team. I love the disadvantaged; they're the reason I joined the Bureau of Harm Reduction. To give them a voice and protect them from people like you taking advantage of them."

UW had joined them while the gray suit was responding and signed to Jack, "Tell him he's an ass."

"He already knows," Jack signed back. "He has to know, right?"

His uncle's chuckle evoked a panicked string of questions from the gray suit. "What did you say to him? Are you making fun of me? Tell me what you said!"

His reaction told Jack all he needed to know. Gray suit was an insecure little man. He imagined him on the playground being picked on and bullied. Gray suit hadn't joined the BHR to help the disadvantaged; he'd joined for revenge against his childhood enemies. Against the monsters still haunting his dreams. His position granted him power, and he intended to lord it over everyone that had wronged him.

In his twisted logic, everyone who succeeded in life had done so at his expense. They were the reason he'd never achieved greatness; they were the reason he was a failure. It made him dangerous.

"Relax," Jack said. "I told him he was working for free. Just busting his chops. Let's review those specs you told me about. I'm ready to get to work."

UW broke from them as they entered the office area and headed into the shop, leaving Jack and Gray Suit alone.

"Hey," Jack said, "what's your name? It was never on the Form 85OI-Observer Integration documents. And you and your partner never introduced yourselves. If we're going to be partners, I should know your name."

The gray suit regarded him suspiciously before answering. "My name is Loomis Crestwater the Third. Call me Agent Crestwater, and only Agent Crestwater. My partner is no longer assigned to Stinger Machinery. He was having difficulty following Agent Woods' directions. As a result, she reassigned him to our camp in the Mojave. Dreadful place."

"Well, good to finally put a name to the face, Agent Crestwater." Jack's face hurt from the smile he'd been faking for the last thirty minutes. But he sure as hell noticed Crestwater's body go stiff when he mentioned the camp in the Mojave. It was clear Jack wasn't supposed to know about it.

"Actually, *Mister* Stinger, knowing my name is rather unimportant. I anticipate moving on to my next assignment as soon as we get this operation back on track. The improvements I've implemented have produced efficiencies unattainable under your management. It's to be expected. I am a Harvard graduate after all."

"Harvard, you say. Impressive. I bet you came up with some humdingers. Can't wait to see them. Hope they're not too good, or we'll have to keep you from being reassigned."

As Crestwater ignored Jack's praise and fumbled through a stack of spec-data sheets looking for the new product information, Randy and Armin walked into the office. Randy made a beeline to Jack and nearly crushed him in a bear hug.

Armin's toothy grin, visible to Jack over Randy's massive shoulder, forced a strained chuckle from Jack.

"Good to see you too," he signed after Randy released him. "Do me a favor. If you have something important to tell me, say it with sign language." And gave a slight nod of his head in the Observer's direction.

Randy and Armin nodded their confirmation as Randy glared at Crestwater.

After an awkward silence, Agent Crestwater finally glanced up from the spec-data sheets and said, "Time to execute your vocation, gentlemen. Dismissed."

Randy looked to Armin and rolled his eyes when Armin translated the message. With a shake of his head, he turned and walked towards the machine shop.

"Ah, here they are!" Agent Crestwater exclaimed.

Jack's eyes went wide when he realized what he was looking at. "Agent Crestwater, when did we start manufacturing guns? M4A1s, to be exact? I'm sure you're aware that Stinger Machinery doesn't hold an 07-FFL."

"Oh, *Mister* Stinger, I told you I've implemented several changes. Our license was issued last week. We simply lack the knowledge necessary to transition our machines to manufacture our new product."

"Huh, that sure is an improvement I didn't see coming. Tell me, who are we manufacturing them for?"

Crestwater was interrupted by Armin screaming from the shop area. Jack sprinted from the office and crashed through the door.

He searched the expansive area for his friend and found him leaning over the tool head of the new CNC machine. "What happened?" he barked. "Are you okay?"

Armin met Jack's stare with rage-filled eyes. "Jack, they haven't been using any cutting lubricant."

"That explains what I saw during my visit," Jack said.

"That's one of my improvements," Agent Crestwater announced proudly. "Much better for the environment."

"The cutting head's been destroyed, and the shaft has seized. We're talking thousands of dollars in parts and man-hours to repair it. What were you using for coolant?"

Crestwater appeared shocked by the news. "I was assured it wouldn't be a problem. The shop steward said cutting lubricant was unnecessary. And I have no idea what coolant is, let alone the type being used. I can assure you that I've seen no purchase order requests for something called coolant."

Jack's head snapped in Agent Crestwater's direction. "Are you kidding me?" he said. "Understand this—if they ruined this machine, it's coming out of your ass, *partner*."

Agent Crestwater stepped away from Jack. "*Mister* Stinger, sadly, I'm not surprised by your Neanderthal-inspired threat. But it is uncalled for. We will address your concerns with the union steward upon his arrival."

As if on cue, the shop door swung open as a group of half a dozen men dressed in filthy gray coveralls sauntered in.

"Crestwater, what the hell's he doing here?" a bearded man screeched while pointing at Jack.

"Really, you're still mad?" Jack offered with his vinyl smile creasing his features.

Scraggly Beard fixed Jack in his best tough-guy glare. "You're lucky the po-po showed up, pal. I was fix'n to open a can of whoop-ass on ya."

"I suppose I am lucky," Jack said. "Hopefully, we can put aside our differences and get some work done."

Randy, who'd been inspecting his machine at the far end of the shop, suddenly appeared behind the group of men. Their posture prompted him to ask Jack if everything was alright.

"We're good. Just playing the game," Jack signed as he saw Randy caressing the handle of a heavy rebar rod fixed in the big man's tool belt.

Confused by Jack's action, the men looked to see who he was motioning to. The sight of Randy's hulking form caused them to scamper away from him and closer to Jack.

Agent Crestwater stepped in front of Jack and yelled, "All of you, everyone in this shop, need to relax. We have a tight timeline, and this bickering only serves to delay our progress."

Armin and UW had shouldered up to Jack, prepared to defend him.

"Hey guys, we're playing the game," he started, using sign language. "So we do as Crestwater asked and relax."

"What's going on, Jack?" Armin's hands flew through the words rapidly. "I'm not okay with what I'm seeing."

"Neither am I. And we're taking our lives back, one step at a time!"

Randy had been watching the exchange between Jack and Armin. "I'm in. Whatever your plan is, I'm in," he signed, grinning.

As the bearded man led the others into the shop, Agent Crestwater exited. With tensions deescalating, Jack motioned for Randy to join him with Armin and UW. They huddled up and Jack told them about the spec-data sheets Crestwater had shared. "We're going to find out why the hell Stinger Machinery is manufacturing military-grade weapons."

Jack noticed Willis give a slight nod toward Randy and Armin. Even though he knew both men from his time at Stinger Machinery, his uncle didn't trust anyone and had just asked Jack if they could trust his long-time employees. Jack felt his anger rise at the accusation, but he realized UW had a point. A lot had changed over the last couple of months.

"Armin, Randy, meet me in my office in five. I need to talk to you." His request received nods of confirmation from both.

Jack turned to UW. "We need to talk, now."

***

Jack and UW had been huddled together a couple of minutes when Scraggly Beard took notice. "Jesus H, how many deaf people are we going to hire? I can't stand this. It makes me uncomfortable, and it's a safety issue."

Jack's spine went stiff. "If you say that again, I'll shove pencils into your eardrums. When I finish, you'll join the deaf people that work here. Have I been clear?"

"Listen up, pal," Scraggly said. "I'm the union steward of this shop. I have a duty to ensure the safety of our union members. Fire them, or we walk."

His back to the loudmouth, Jack said, "Be careful the door doesn't hit your ass on your way out."

It was a risky move, but he hedged his bet that the other union members needed their jobs. The country was shut down, and the government stipend trickling out wouldn't be enough to cover their liquor bill, let alone put food on the table.

"That's it! Let's go, boys. We aren't safe in this second-rate rat hole." He stormed towards the door with one of his crew in tow. He stopped at the exit and spun to find the other men powering on their machines. "What the hell? I called a strike. Move your asses. This is about solidarity. We're a brotherhood."

A wiry man whose coveralls appeared two sizes too big spoke up. "Alex, union bylaws mandate a vote for strikes. I vote no."

Alex flushed crimson with anger. "I said get your asses moving. We hold the power. Time to use it."

The man again voiced his no vote, sending Alex into full-tilt. "OKAY, all in favor of striking, raise your hand." He and the only man that had followed him raised their hands. The rest stared blankly.

"Whatever. I'm leaving. I have the flu!" Alex screamed.

Jack, flashing a smug grin, said, "Don't forget to punch out as you leave. Feel better soon."

He waited until the door slammed before restarting the conversation with UW. "So, Lisa's safe? How did you avoid the BHR finding her, and why?"

UW smiled. "I don't know why I did it; had the same feeling you did. The less the government knows, the better."

Crestwater cut Willis off when he stuck his head through the door and yelled for Jack to join him in his office.

"Well, Crestwater just figured out that two of his worker bees left the hive. I'll swing back around after I talk to Randy and Armin." Jack paused, taking in the chaotic mess of the shop area. "Can you get this mess cleaned up?"

UW nodded, and Jack headed for the office.

He was dismayed to find Crestwater sitting in the office adjoining his. The man would be able to keep tabs on Jack every second he spent in the cramped space. "You wanted to see me, partner?"

"*Mister* Stinger, can you explain why two of our team stormed from the premises less than an hour into the workday? I thought I was clear that our timeline was such that we needed every available body toiling away at a machine."

"Agent Crestwater, they insulted the hearing-impaired members of our team. Something I will not tolerate."

"Ah, yes, that brings me to my next question," Crestwater said. "According to Willis Stinger's last medical update, when he retired five years ago..." Crestwater hadn't looked up from the file he was viewing. "No hearing impairment was mentioned. How do you explain that?"

"You weren't kidding when you said you'd be vetting the people I brought back." Jack was stalling. The question had caught him off guard. "Well, it happened gradually over the last couple of years. He was too damn stubborn to see a doctor. When he finally did, it was too late. Doctor blamed his time serving in the military. I guess all the noise the machines of freedom make took their toll."

Crestwater glanced up from the folder. "A real American Hero. Raining death onto the heads of children around the globe."

Jack knew the comment's purpose. He wasn't about to give Agent Crestwater the satisfaction. "Well, you can check with his doctors if you'd like; they'll confirm it," Jack answered with his plastic smile on full display.

Daring Agent Crestwater to dig further into UW's medical history was a gamble, one he had to take.

"I may do that. Until then, I'd like you to translate the conversations you have with Willis and the other one… Randy, that's his name, correct?"

Jack nodded his confirmation.

"I thought so. Anyway, I'll need transcripts of your conversations with the hearing-impaired members of our team. Deliver them nightly and place them in the center of my desk. I'll review them each morning. Use twelve-point font with double spacing."

"Do you prefer a specific type of font?" Jack asked jokingly.

"I prefer Courier New. But I'll simplify it for you. Use the current default."

Agent Crestwater's beady, dark eyes locked Jack in a mocking stare, goading him to lash out.

"Courier New it is." Jack nodded. "Anything else?"

"Yes, figure out how we replace the men that left us today."

"Well," Jack said. "If the condition of our shop is any indication, we're better off without them. I'll talk to the men. We'll have the shop running at full capacity by mid-afternoon. Except the CNC lathe. Armin's inspecting it. Depending on what he finds, it could be down for a while. And we'll be switching back to standard lubricants. Unless you'd like to extend the timeline? Your call, partner."

"Do whatever it takes. Just get those machines working!"

"I will. But, what is our timeline? You've mentioned it's tight, but I need to know. How tight is it?"

"Mid-October, *Mister* Stinger. We must manufacture four thousand rifles by mid-October."

Jack's head tilted. "That's impossible, Agent Crestwater. It's already April, and unless you plan to operate twenty-four seven, we'll never hit that number by mid-October."

"I'm aware of the challenge, JACK," Crestwater screeched as he interrupted him. "You have one job: Get those machines running!"

Chapter 38

Peter Mathews' Home

Mathews made his way to the security camera he'd set up to monitor the 85 Plumbing van parked in the street. It had become his daily routine as he tracked the van's activity.

He'd noticed a pattern developing over the last several days. At exactly 3 a.m. each morning, a shift change took place. Three people in tactical clothing arrived in a dark-colored sedan, tapped the van's rear door twice, and were let in. Exactly seven minutes later, an equal number of tactically dressed operators exited the van and drove off in the sedan.

He had expected the 85 Plumbing van to disappear after they finished their gun confiscation operation in the neighborhood. But it hadn't. And after Willis told him about the listening devices he and his nephew found in their homes, he understood why. He had found none in his home, but he was sure they were there. He'd been living in silence ever since. Well, except for playing ear-splitting music occasionally.

As he neared the window, the sound of voices reached him, causing his pace to quicken. He was stunned to see dozens of people gathered across the street in Lincoln Park. It appeared a festival-like event was taking place. Half a dozen small canopy booths were set up, forming a perimeter around the gathering, each with tables full of food manned by smiling gray-suited attendants. A small raised platform anchored the far edge of the event grounds. The entire area was ringed by armed guards standing watch, with MP5s hanging from single-point slings.

He watched as groups of civilians wandered from booth to booth, filling plates with whatever was being offered. At each stop, a gray suit would engage them in conversation while some handed out flyers.

"What the actual hell?" Mathews whispered. He was careful not to disturb the curtains as he watched through the small gap. After several moments, he began recognizing some of the civilian attendees from his neighborhood. Even Thatcher and Margaux joined the growing crowd.

"You two really don't own any other clothing, do you?" He laughed softly.

Movement near the raised platform caught his attention. A group of guards was clustered together to the left of the small structure. A moment later, they parted, allowing a tall, gray-suited man to step onto the platform.

The man raised his arms and yelled something unintelligible to the crowd. Mathews decided to find out what was happening and bolted downstairs, intent on joining the festivities.

He was standing next to the 85 Plumbing truck a flash later and drew the attention of one of the guards.

"Can I help you, sir?" a young woman asked while bringing her MP5 to low ready and moving toward him.

"You must have forgotten to send me an invitation. I'm here for the food; see what the hullabaloo's about," Mathews answered. "And how about relaxing that gun. You took mine, remember? I'm harmless now."

"Sir, where's your essential person badge? You're to display it at all times."

"You mean where are my *papers?*" Mathews responded. "Check with whoever's in the van. I'm sure they can tell you where I live *and* my essential status."

The guard's eyes went squinty with suspicion. "Return to your resident dwelling immediately." She reached for her shoulder-mounted radio.

"This is a public park," Mathews said, gesturing at the area behind her. "My tax dollars pay for its upkeep. I've helped clean it up more than once. I'm allowed to be here... with or without my papers, *comrade.*"

Mathews hadn't heard what the guard said into her radio, but it became clear as two additional guards moved in his direction with weapons at high-ready. This wouldn't end well for him.

"Sir, return to your resident dwelling," a second guard ordered.

"You all need to relax. I'm allowed to be outside of my *resident dwelling*. Plus, I want some of that food." His sarcastic grin was on full display.

The guards twisted around as someone yelled, "Lock the pig up!"

Mathews followed their stares to find Thatcher's smiling face.

"Lock him up, lock him up." The rest of the crowd quickly added their voices to his chant.

Mob mentality quickly spread, emboldening Thatcher to approach Mathews. His chest puffed to his thin frame's extent, he stopped before breaching the safety of the guards' perimeter.

"You're a murderer! An oppressor of the disadvantaged and underprivileged. You should be locked away forever. Purged from existence!" He raised his fist above his head in a show of solidarity with the mob forming behind him.

The guards didn't appear as threatened by the angry throng as they had with Mathews' mere presence and lowered their weapons.

"You're shitting me, right?" he questioned the guards.

The female guard opened her mouth to answer, but the tall man on the podium yelled to the crowd, cutting her off.

"Citizen Soldiers, the first virtue you must embrace is patience. You must learn to look past the vile crust of our enemy if you wish to change his heart."

An unsettling silence fell over the crowd as the tall man said with a snake-oil smile, "You there, what's your name?"

It took Mathews a second to realize the man was speaking to him. "None-ya," he said. "As in none-ya fucking business! And what exactly is a citizen soldier?"

The tall man's smile faltered ever so slightly, then returned at fifty thousand candle strength. "I see you're holding tight to the old ways, the destructive ways. You should join us in our fight against oppressors and terrorists, become a citizen soldier."

As he spoke, several guards hoisted a banner over his head. Mathews stared incredulously at the words: "Citizen Soldiers, Cleveland, Ohio Chapter."

"I can see you're impressed with our banner. But you'll be more impressed with the benefits that accompany membership."

Mathews never took his eyes from the banner as he spoke. "Impressed? That's one way to put it. Tell me something, isn't it too dangerous to be in public? Or do the terrorists ignore citizen soldiers?"

The man's patience evaporated as Mathews spoke. "Fine, return to your pathetic little world. Your hateful, miserable existence." He shifted to address the crowd. "Remember him, soldiers. Burn his face into your memory. He represents all we fight against. Mark my words: We will wipe him and his ilk from our country. And when we finish, we will be free to live our lives as normal."

Mathews was thrown by the crowd's reaction; they cheered and applauded the tall man's proclamation. He glanced around and realized all that was missing were brown shirts and swastikas.

The crowd's enthusiasm grew, prompting Mathews to take a step back. They massed behind the guards who were now smiling at him. Without a gun, he wouldn't stand a chance if they rushed him, so he headed back towards his home. He locked eyes with Thatcher and nodded while mouthing a message: "Your time is coming."

***

Safely locked in his home, he stared through the window as the tall man regained control of the zealots. He had delivered his message, and Mathews heard it loud and clear.

He grabbed his gov-issued phone and dialed his old precinct. A voice he didn't recognize answered. "This is Officer Mathews, retired. I'm calling to report an unlawful and violent gathering in Lincoln Park."

"Sir, we are aware of the citizen soldier rally. It is peaceful and poses no threat to you or the participants."

"Who am I speaking to?" Mathews barked. "Actually, I don't care. Put the shift commander on the line."

After a brief pause, the line was picked up. "This is Shift Commander Ellis. And I assure you, the rally is safe. Our guards are currently onsite and have reported only one disturbance. Seems a dissident tried to rile up the crowd. But *we* dealt with him. Hopefully, he's smart enough to remain in his resident dwelling."

Mathews could hear the man's smile through the phone. He disconnected the call with a curse and grabbed his sat-phone. After powering it on, he typed two words. "Accelerated timeline."

CHAPTER 39

STINGER MACHINERY

Jack scowled as he reviewed the numbers for Stinger Machinery. Three weeks into his partnership with the BHR, it had become clear that the government should never run a business. They applied the same financial responsibility to private industry as they had with tax dollars. They spent every dime, then borrowed more.

Stinger Machinery's material vendors were billing them three times what he'd been paying at the end of the previous year. More concerning was the quality; particularly, the chrome-moly bar stock used for the barrels. It was arriving out of spec and wasn't holding up to the cutting process used to add the rifling. It was bad enough that he demanded the Stinger Machinery manufacturer's stamp be removed from the finished product.

They hadn't shipped a single finished rifle, nor had he created a single invoice. This couldn't continue.

He leaned back in his chair and stared at the ceiling, wondering again how this had happened, when his phone rang, breaking his thought. His favorite Bureau of Harm Reduction agent was calling.

"This is Jack Stinger. How may I help you, Agent Woods."

"*Mister* Stinger, your tone tells me that things are progressing nicely. Is my observation accurate?"

Jack stuffed what he wanted to say, opting instead to tell her what she wanted to hear. "Yes, moving along nicely. Everyone is committed to the plan and happy to be employed. Speaking of employees, how are we paying them?"

The sound of shuffling paper preceded her reply. "Their earnings are being distributed by direct deposit. Why, has someone missed a paycheck?"

"That wasn't my question. We haven't generated a red cent of revenue. How is Stinger meeting payroll?"

"Your government is very resourceful. So don't you fret, Stinger Machinery's obligations are being met."

Jack waited for Agent Woods to share the details. When she didn't, he broke the awkward silence. "I'm sure you had something else you wished to talk about. So, what can I do for you?"

"Very perceptive, *Mister* Stinger. Despite our best efforts, we still haven't located your wife. Her phone remains unused, as do the funds in her Omni-Online account. Do you have any information? Have you been in contact with her?"

Jack shifted uneasily in his chair. "I haven't," he answered in a somber voice. "I miss her terribly. Do you think she's...?"

"Don't think like that." The genuine concern in her voice brought a smile to his face. "I'm sure she's just fine. Probably taking her time sorting through her feelings. Trying to determine how to move forward. Matters of the heart can be complex. We'll find her."

"Thank you, Agent Woods," Jack answered, his trembling voice worthy of an Academy Award. "Please keep me posted on your progress."

"You'll be the first person I call. Good day."

Jack blew air through puffed cheeks, pondering how long he'd be able to keep up his charade when movement from his office's doorway drew his attention. He found the wiry man who'd stood up to the union steward a few weeks ago staring back at him.

"What's the word?" he asked.

Billy fidgeted while glancing nervously behind him. "This is for you," he whispered, stepping forward and dropping a folded piece of paper on Jack's desk. "I want to let you know, things are going great." This time, he practically yelled the words.

Jack's confusion gave way to understanding as Agent Crestwater seemed to materialize behind Billy. "Can we help you, Billy?"

Startled by Agent Crestwater's question and sudden appearance, Billy flinched. "I guess I should tell you too, things are running smooth in the shop these days."

Jack caught the man's reaction and stealthily covered the folded paper with a manila folder. "Good to hear, Billy. Thanks for sharing."

Billy nodded confirmation at Jack as the agent ordered him to get back to work.

"When will they learn their place?" Agent Crestwater asked, frustration lacing his words.

"Meh, no problem. He just wants to be part of the team that's building something important. Something our government needs. It's a good sign. Means our team is gelling, and that means production will increase."

Agent Crestwater appeared shocked by Jack's statement. Mired in hierarchal division, he wasn't comfortable with management and the worker bees mingling. "Still, abandoning his post during non-break times is unacceptable. Should we dock his pay?"

"Sure, you do that. Dock a man's pay for ten whole minutes. Let me know how it goes when his union gets involved. Then, when production drops, you can request an extension on the timeline. By the way, he machines the trigger group assemblies." Jack locked Agent Crestwater in a hard stare. "Or, you can accept the compliment he felt needed to be delivered to management. Something which rarely happens. Your call."

"This trigger group assembly you speak of. Is it essential?"

Jack dragged a hand down his face. "The boom-stick won't go boom without it." Addressing Agent Crestwater's quizzical stare, he clarified, "The gun will NOT fire a bullet without a trigger assembly. It is essential. Actually, all the parts of a firearm are essential. So we need him, and every man we have, running those machines."

Crestwater appeared surprised, and Jack figured the man had been scheming ways to streamline the production process with the sole intent of hitting the timeline. All of which involved removing the more laborious parts from the guns.

"Agent Crestwater, the bitterness of poor quality remains long after the sweetness of meeting the schedule has faded."

"That's not an accurate quote," Crestwater offered. "I believe it should be…"

"I know what Benjamin Franklin said. But it's no less true. All the parts of the boom-stick will be manufactured and assembled to craft the best possible boom-stick. Have I been clear?"

"Yes, clear." Unhappy with Jack's dismissive tone, Crestwater attempted to gain control of the conversation. "Speaking of poor quality. I'm disappointed with the summaries of your conversations with the hearing-impaired members of our team."

"In what way," Jack interrupted.

"They seem abbreviated, perfunctory, even. I've observed your interactions, and your communications appear quite complex. Are you relaying them to me in their entirety?"

"Perfunctory? Huh, I've never been accused of that," Jack said. "Agent Crestwater, I will not debate the finer points of sign language with you. If you don't trust my summaries to be accurate or truthful, I suggest you take a class on communicating with the deaf. It'll be an eye-opener. Now, I'm going to the shop to check on their progress. Care to join me?"

The agent hadn't stepped foot in the shop area since the day Jack had returned. Actually, he'd avoided even walking past the door. It was where the worker bees were. He couldn't be seen mingling with riffraff. He made a moue of distaste.

Jack ended the awkward silence. "Okay then. Let me know what you decide about Billy."

***

Jack detoured into the men's room and pulled Billy's note from between the files he'd scooped from his desk as he exited his office. The message caught Jack off guard: "I'm in."

Panic raced through him. Billy knew what they were planning. How?

Jack was in the shop, standing next to Billy, before he realized his legs were moving. The slightly built man gave him a nervous nod, then glanced around the shop. Satisfied that everyone was sufficiently distracted by their work, he powered down his machine and smiled. "My brother's deaf. Oh, and I hate Eden. It was a mistake voting for him."

Jack's head went light. Billy had been "eavesdropping" on his conversations. He'd understood everything! This man held Jack's future, his very life, in his hands. Then it hit him. If Billy intended to spy on them, he'd have kept his mouth shut. Hell, he already knew enough to have Jack, UW, Armin, and Randy arrested.

Jack chuckled and shook his head. "I hate the bastard too."

After his twenty-minutes-long conversation with Billy, Jack walked through the shop area under UW's questioning stare. As he reached the exit, he signed to his uncle to meet him in his office during his break.

***

"Do you trust him?"

"Billy knows everything. He knows about Lisa, our sat-phones, the guns. He knows enough to have already turned us in for a huge reward from the BHR. UW, I think we have to trust him. Or at least let him believe we do."

"I can't believe we let this happen," UW said. "We were sloppy. But, we may be able to turn it around. You said he has unrestricted status?" Jack nodded in confirmation. "Okay, pump him for information. Find out what he knows about this citizen soldier bullshit. How're the BHR recruiting them, their base of operations, force size, any intelligence will be helpful."

His uncle paused, and Jack watched as the military man transformed into a battlefield commander. "From what Mathews told me, it sounds like the classic divide and conquer. He said, if his memory wasn't failing him, the people he recognized attending the rally in Lincoln Park had Eden campaign signs in their yards during the election. I'm not sure how much stock I put in his recall. He's taken an abundance of blows to the head, but it seems plausible."

Jack chuckled at the comment. "Didn't he mention something about holding the CPD record for being punched in the face?"

UW joined in the laughter as he nodded. "He does. Plus, he's former Army infantry. Those boys take a beating."

As the laughter trailed off, the realization of the dangers associated with what they were planning set in. The close call with Billy made it perfectly clear.

"Are we doing the right thing?"

"There's never been a righter thing," UW signed as he smiled.

Chapter 40

Stinger Machinery Delivery Van

Two weeks had passed since Billy asked to be a part of the plan. His boss continued to keep him at arm's length. He understood Jack's reasoning. Rumors of *enlightenment* camps established in the Mojave and Sonora deserts had circulated during the citizen soldier meetings Billy had attended. He figured the rumors were true and being spread to keep the populace obedient to the whim of government, or more accurately, the combined whims of the Bureaus of Harm Reduction and Civic Responsibility. The latter of which was tasked with running the desert facilities.

But today he'd prove himself worthy of Jack's trust. The thought made him smile.

"What's so funny, Billy? Do I amuse you?" Agent Crestwater asked.

Billy, caught off guard, quickly recovered. "It's good to see we're getting back to normal," he offered while motioning towards the van's windshield to a lone, panic-stricken, woman rushing through the intersection where they waited for the light to change. "Do you think we finally put the terrorists out of business?"

From the passenger seat, Crestwater appeared annoyed with Billy's observation. "No, I do not believe we've *put them out of business.* I believe they are lying in wait for us to lower our guard. We won't know true safety until we've dealt with every single dissident. The people scurrying about, yourself included, were granted freedoms based on loyalty. But we must remain vigilant, even with them, *and you.* It takes but one nonconformist whispering in a sympathetic ear to form the first crack in our defenses. That's the reason Jack isn't delivering our payload. Even *he* can't be trusted."

Crestwater was cut off when a horn honked behind them. Billy had been so stunned by the agent's statement he'd failed to notice the light had changed to green. With more pressure than he'd intended, Billy stepped on the gas, causing the van's wheels to chirp in response.

"BILLY, do I need to remind you of our cargo? If you damaged a single gun because you're incompetent, I will hold you personally responsible."

Billy cursed his carelessness. He couldn't give Crestwater a reason to inspect all the guns when they delivered them to the civilian soldiers' headquarters. After apologizing, he said a silent prayer that the crates hadn't shifted.

Billy was thankful for quiet during their drive to the converted gun range which served as the civilian soldiers' headquarters. The silence allowed him to review the plan and form contingencies if things went sideways. By the time he backed the van to the loading bay, he'd imagined every scenario from a full-blown shoot-out to a simple handshake. The latter being his preference.

His hopes were dashed as a giant of a man he'd never noticed at the civilian soldier meetings met him at the van's cargo doors.

"You the one testing the guns?" The man's grin told him it wasn't a question.

It suddenly became clear why the citizen soldiers had chosen a shooting range for their headquarters. "Sure, load up a few magazines. I'm looking forward to it. I'll pretend it's one of the terrorists I'm shooting."

"Nice touch," the man growled while nodding his approval. "I'll set up while you grab a sample."

Relief spread through Billy as the man walked away with Crestwater in tow. He grabbed the crate with the scarcely noticeable "85" written in its upper left corner and lugged it into the range area. "I'll unload the rest, and then we get to the fun part."

"Don't worry about unloading. Our boys can handle that. Let's get shooting."

"Nah, Stinger Machinery's a full-service operation. Let me know where you want them." Billy prayed they didn't notice the sweat tricking down the sides of his face.

"Suit yourself," Giant-Man said. "But we need to record the serial numbers and inspect them. So you may be awhile."

"They've been function tested twice, and each packing slip lists the serial numbers," Billy responded, struggling to keep the panic out of his voice. "I'll leave the packing slips with your admin, if that's alright with you?"

Billy thought he caught suspicion flash across the man's features before Agent Crestwater interjected. "Russell, we're running a top-notch operation. The crate's contents were carefully packed and accurately accounted for. Let Billy unload so he can begin testing them. I have something to talk to you about before he begins. It'll afford us the privacy needed for the conversation."

Russell gave a stiff nod. "Deliver them to the armory, around the corner." He pointed to a narrow hallway. "Be sure to lock the door after you've finished," he yelled over his shoulder.

Billy moved quickly to unload the rest of the crates from the van and move them to the armory. The amount of firepower he found already stored behind the armory's heavy steel door made it clear that Stinger Machinery wasn't the only business supplying the civilian soldiers with rifles. And, as with Stinger Machinery's heavy wooden crates, none of them displayed identifying markings. The only link to their manufacturer was the rifles' serial numbers.

After mixing Stinger's rifle crates with the ones already there, he pulled the serial number list from each. "Have fun with this useless information," he smirked.

Twenty minutes later, Billy slammed the armory door and secured the padlock. He stood there for a moment, trying to calm himself before rejoining Crestwater and Russell. He wasn't in the clear yet.

***

"Took you long enough," Russell snipped as Billy joined him and Crestwater in the range. "Your eye and ear protection are on the shelf. Send thirty rounds through each of the three M4s in that crate. I want to see them function in semi-auto and three-round bursts. We'll be watching from the Range Officers' observation area, directly behind you. If you experience a malfunction, keep the gun pointed downrange and signal to me to join you. Have I been clear?"

Billy nodded his understanding as he slipped on the protective gear. Feigning confusion, he fumbled with the gun's controls, flipping it back and forth until he found what he was looking for: a small "x" engraved on the bottom of the trigger guard. Relieved, he slapped the magazine into the mag-well and pressed the bolt carrier release. *Please work,* he thought as he lined up his sights and pulled the trigger.

The powerful 5.56 rounds punished Billy's shoulder when he selected three-round burst. He smiled. It'd been years since he'd held a rifle; he'd sworn them off the same time he'd switched political parties. And had just realized how much he'd regretted it.

When the last round slammed into the backstop, he checked the chamber and yelled, "Clear. Range is no longer hot."

Russell was the first to join him, and the giant-man's smile told him he was pleased with the test.

"You're a decent shot. You have formal training?"

Billy faced Russell, noticing, for the first time, the jagged scar running the length of his forehead. "Dad used to take me hunting when I was a kid. Honestly, I hate guns. They make me uncomfortable."

Russell's booming laugh confused Billy. "What'd I say?"

Giant-Man wiped at his eyes while shaking his head. "You're not the only one that feels that way."

Billy's confusion cleared as Crestwater finally joined them on the firing line, holding a notepad in front of his crotch. He noticed the dark stain running down the agent's pants leg a moment later.

"Your boss pissed himself when you fired the first round. I've never seen anyone jump and twitch so much in my life." Russell wiped at his eyes again. "He screamed so loud I thought you shot him."

Russell's laughter boomed in the background as Agent Crestwater turned crimson, his features vacillating between humiliation and rage. "It's time to go, Billy."

"I think we have some diapers in storage. They should fit!" Russell bellowed as Crestwater and Billy entered the van.

***

Agent Crestwater bolted to his Prius the instant Billy pulled into a parking space. He rolled down the window and shouted, "I'll be back after a quick stop at my apartment. Not a word of this incident. I'm suffering a touch of PTSD after being exposed to those gawdawful weapons. Enduring additional humiliation at the hands of the brutes in that building may cause a complete mental breakdown. One requiring hospitalization."

Billy's blank stare prompted Crestwater to elaborate. "If I'm not here to monitor progress and implement efficiencies, it could jeopardize the entire project."

Billy nodded his understanding. "Mum's the word."

***

Tears streamed down Jack's cheeks as Billy relayed the story of Crestwater's accident, via sign language, and away from the prying eyes of the BHR shop workers. UW, Armin, and Randy were bright red with laughter.

As the levity faded, Jack met Billy's expectant stare. "You did good, Billy. We've asked a lot of you, and you've met the challenge head-on. UW has something for you. He'll bring it tomorrow."

Billy's smile was infectious as UW gave him a congratulatory slap on the back.

CHAPTER 41

RAVEN ROCK MOUNTAIN MILITARY COMPLEX

Vice President Genus paced the plush carpeting of Raven Rocks' expansive conference room. Her fingernails had been chewed to nubs as panic gripped her. Initially ecstatic about Eden falling ill and imagining her name etched in history as the first female President of the United States, her dreams of glory were doused in the frigid water of reality in the months that had passed.

She glanced at the pile of intelligence reports sitting atop the conference room table, demanding her attention, and realized she was wholly unprepared to be the leader of the free world. Stuck in this hellhole with no aides or advisers to rely on or blame, she found herself running the country, alone.

"This is completely unacceptable!" she screamed.

In response to her outburst, two Secret Service agents rushed into the room, guns drawn, searching for a threat. Instead, they found the Vice President spinning in a circle and staring at the ceiling.

"Vice President Genus? Can we help you? Are you okay?" one agent asked.

Visibly startled, Genus turned her mascara-streaked face towards the agents. "Do I look okay?" she responded just above a whisper. "The whole damn world is falling apart, and somehow I'm supposed to put it back together. It's all on me. ON MY SHOULDERS!"

The agents stood in stunned silence, unsure of how to respond.

"Don't just stand there for God's sake. Call my doctor. Tell her I need my medication."

The agents holstered their weapons but didn't move.

Voice trembling, Genus exploded. "I gave you a direct order. Are you deaf or stupid? If you're too ignorant to follow orders, I'll find someone who can."

The agent closest to her smiled. "Vice President Genus, take a seat."

Her confusion mounted as the second agent turned, closed the door to the conference room, then took a defensive position in front of it. "My partner asked you to be seated."

"Excuse me, Agent, whatever your name is. To whom do you think you're speaking?"

"SIT DOWN!" the agent closest to her screamed.

Genus' eyes went wide as she stumbled to a chair. "You're them, the terrorists, aren't you?"

As she lowered herself into the chair, she became vaguely aware of a phone ringing somewhere in the room. She jumped when one of the agents began speaking. "Yes, sir, I believe she's ready. I'll pull up the video feed. What's that? Yes, of course the room is secure."

The agent walked to the conference room's control center and typed a series of commands into the keyboard. A flash later, the massive monitor blazed to life.

"You're going to broadcast my execution to the world, aren't you? You sick bastards," Genus screeched through her uncontrolled sobbing.

Her attention focused on the agent working the control center, she yelped when a voice sprang from the monitors' speakers. "Vice President Genus, wonderful to see you."

She turned to face the monitor and found Chief of Staff Roberts' smug visage filling every pixel of the screen.

"No, this is not your execution. Not that you'd be missed if it were."

"What's the meaning of this, Roberts?" she said, her voice strained from fear and confusion.

"I'm your lifeline, Madam President." Roberts chuckled at Genus' confusion. "You didn't think I'd let you run this country by yourself, did you? That's so cute; like a small child helping Mommy bake cookies. They too think they're actually useful. When, in fact, if left to their own devices, they'd burn the house to ash. I'm in control, Genus. Not you. Nary a thing you've done wasn't approved by me first. And, you'll be relieved to hear that you may discontinue reviewing your intelligence reports. I've taken action on each long before they reach your desk."

Swallowing her emotions, Genus fixed him in as an intimidating stare as she could muster. "Check your tone, Roberts. I'm still the Vice President and demand the respect that accompanies my office."

Roberts' hysterical laughter boomed through the conference room. "You see. That's the problem. You're so preoccupied with your station in life, you've missed my message. I'll clarify: Genus, you are useless, an empty suit. When your mouth opens, the world cringes. That's why I've been in command. Yes, that is what I said; I'm running things, not you or Eden. Me. But of course let's focus on our words and how we use them. They're far more important than the message... idiot!"

Roberts watched as the worry straining Genus' features disappeared. She wiped away the mascara-stained tears and smiled tremulously. He recognized her reaction. Relief.

"I'm pleased to see you understand." He nodded. "We're a team, you and I. And our team has much to accomplish."

"Put me in, Coach." The statement was followed by her signature cackle.

"Our initial order of business is to rid you of that, that thing you call a laugh. The second is to ensure we script every word leaving your mouth. If successful, we may mitigate instances where you say things like *put me in, Coach.*"

Roberts resisted the urge to order the Secret Service agents to shoot her when she replied with a salute and a beaming smile.

"Genus, you must understand that the world is watching. The American people are watching. Both seek leadership during these troublesome times. Our allies have enacted similar measures as terroristic activity, similar to what we've experienced, has reared its ugly head in their countries. The world is a powder keg. We must keep the matchhead from igniting the proverbial wick. Have I been clear?"

Genus nodded emphatically. "You've been clear. It's imperative we lead, not follow."

"Verygood,"Robertssaid."Now,what'syourrecommendation for dealing with our members of Congress? They've become increasingly problematic as they receive an ever-increasing number of complaints from their constituencies."

His laughter again filled the speakers when Genus' face filled with terror. "I'm kidding; I know you have no plan. You can barely dress yourself in the morning. However, the situation is serious and one I've given a great deal of thought to. I'll start by informing you of the steps we've already taken. Then we'll move on to determining a more permanent solution."

Roberts referred to his notepad. "We've attempted to ease restrictions on the people by approving more Form 85NEV-Nonessential Visitation requests than originally intended. This is not a permanent solution. We feel it's dangerous to permit the un-vetted to co-mingle until we have a clear picture of the terrorists' capabilities. They've proven quite capable thus far. Allowing them the opportunity to conscript or convert additional dissidents is counterproductive. But, granting the populace some freedoms should pacify them in the short term. However, we must demonstrate our leadership. It's imperative that they see a functioning government."

Roberts glanced at his buzzing phone, then set it down while rolling his eyes. "Speak of the devil," he murmured. "Forgive the interruption. The very government officials we speak of are calling me non-stop. Anyway, we've begun recruiting the civilians who have been granted unrestricted essential person status into the ranks of citizen soldiers."

Genus perked at the mention of citizen soldiers. "That was my idea. I'm glad I was able to contribute."

Roberts' face rested in his palm. "No, it wasn't your idea. Your speech merely mentioned them. But I applaud your enthusiasm. As I was saying. The creation of the citizen soldiers should allow us to root out low-threat dissidents while freeing up our intelligence community to locate and eliminate the more serious threats to our republic."

"Where do I sign up for that job?" Genus blurted out, her cackle cut short by Roberts' disapproving glare. "Right, I need to work on that."

"Now, if I may continue," Roberts said. "The flow of intelligence from the Bureau of Harm Reduction after their civil safety raids is ongoing. However, we're sure some groups are flying under our radar. Which brings us back to our original challenge. How do we curtail the movements of the American people while pacifying them and their elected officials?"

Roberts waited for her to answer, but Genus simply stared at him. "That's what I thought. You have nothing to offer. Let me explain our strategy. We've contacted a select group of legacy media to inform them we will grant them the privilege of restarting regular broadcasts. We will script every word of these broadcasts to advance our agenda."

Roberts stopped speaking. Genus wasn't taking any notes, she simply bobbed her head in agreement. "Vice President Genus, do you possess an eidetic memory?"

"A whaaat kind of memory?" Her face scrunched in confusion.

"A photographic memory," Roberts snapped. "You don't, so please take notes. You'll play an active role in our strategy. And I'm not keen to repeat myself."

After she secured a pen and paper, Roberts continued. "I'll handle the heavy lifting with the media. As stated, a select group of media outlets will be granted airtime privileges. I will control their guest list and broadcasts to reflect our goals. You are to convince our members of Congress to gather for a joint session in DC. Ensure them that security will be airtight. You will join them via video link. Your speech will be supplied later. I suspect that wrangling them together under the current circumstances will be difficult and time-consuming. However, you must be successful by early October. I will focus our media strategy on forcing them back to work. Have I been clear?"

"Um, this seems like a lot of work, getting them all together, that is. How do you propose I do that?"

"Your question reveals why I told you to take notes. Have you been listening? Americans need to see their leadership. We will shame Congress using the media. The imbalance of freedoms amongst Americans will increase calls from their constituents. Use these items to force them together." Roberts was practically screaming when he finished.

With a contemptuous glare, he made one last statement. "For the health of you and your family, do not fail."

Roberts disconnected the video feed and smiled as Genus' terrified features disappeared from the monitor. "Fear is a powerful tool."

CHAPTER 42

TWENTY-ONE MONTHS POST INAUGURATION, STINGER MACHINERY

Jack hefted the final crate of M4s into Stinger's delivery van. The sound of traffic filtering from the street on the beautiful October day reminded him of the times before Eden's administration. When his business and his country were prosperous.

Now, he found himself loading weapons he'd manufactured into a van his company could no longer afford. His hopes of turning things around during the summer months were dashed as he watched Stinger Machinery incur hundreds of thousands of dollars in debt the government seemed unconcerned about. His home had slipped into foreclosure, his life savings were all but gone, and he hadn't seen his wife in months. The latter of which would be remedied this evening now that the Bureau of Civic Responsibility had approved his Form 85NEV-Nonessential Visitation request. He shuddered at the realization that he felt happy the government had granted him the freedom to visit family. When in reality, he should be furious about it.

His bitterness honed to a razor's edge, he slammed the door and stood quietly, struggling to tuck his rage away to be visited another day. Pulling a deep breath, he turned to head back into Stinger Machinery and nearly plowed into Billy.

"Shit, you nearly gave me a heart attack!" Jack started, then quickly asked, "Where's your gov-phone?"

Billy smiled. "That hunk of shit is at my workstation; I'll grab it before I leave."

With an approving nod, Jack said, "You ready for this?"

Billy understood Jack's question was deeper than the delivery of M4s. "Yep. They trust me now. Security doesn't give me a second look when I walk in. No one's noticed the serial numbers, and I've made sure they don't use our guns for practice."

Billy had begun removing the serial number documents from the outsides of the other manufactures gun crates on his second delivery and supplying them to Jack. Stinger Machinery then reused those numbers on their guns. The citizen soldiers would eventually figure it out, but the confusion created by their deception would buy Jack and the others valuable time.

"You still their acting firearms training instructor?"

Billy nodded. "Yep, so far. I'm the only one that can hit the target. From what I'm seeing, if the BHR issues these idiots guns, they'll kill themselves before they get out of the building. The only one worrying me is Russell. He's taken several members under his wing, keeps them after our training. I'm not sure what he's up to, but I'll figure it out."

Billy locked eyes with Jack. "You've asked me the same question every day this week. We got this. Relax, Jack. Our line in the sand is deep and well planned. Have faith in your uncle. He knows what he's doing."

The *plan* remained the crux of the issue and Jack's salty mood. They shouldn't need a plan. Not in the United States.

It was something one expected in shithole third-world banana republics. Not America.

He continued praying for a November miracle. Prayed his team would win back the country in a landslide but prepared himself for the inevitable. His blinders were off; they'd pushed him too far.

Snapping from his momentary lapse, he regarded Billy with a grin. "Our line is deep."

***

Jack entered the office to find Agent Crestwater glued to the small television he'd purchased with money Stinger Machinery didn't have.

"I'm thrilled Eden has granted our media the ability to once again broadcast. It feels… normal."

Crestwater's worshipful expression sent a chill down Jack's spine for two reasons. First: only outlets which previously displayed unyielding loyalty to Eden were back on air. Second: they broadcasted pro-Eden propaganda twenty-four hours a day, every day.

He glanced at the television screen. A Congressman Jack didn't recognize appeared to be enduring a harsh line of questioning via video link, which seemed more interrogation than interview. The rotund, balding journalist spat questions at his guest, each dripping with accusation and disdain.

"Oh, my word," Crestwater exclaimed. "Just give up and get your slimy ass back to DC as requested."

It took Jack a tick to realize Agent Crestwater was addressing the Congressman. He nodded in understanding that the journalist's victim held opposing political credentials.

"What's going on?" he asked.

Crestwater faced him, eyes filled with excitement. "The administration has ordered Congress to hold a joint session. As a show of unity in these troublesome times. The representatives sharing *your* ideology feel it's a dangerous proposition. Funny, considering they're the very reason we have these domestic terrorists rampaging through our streets."

Jack's emotional control splintered at Crestwater's statement. "Rampaging through our streets, you say? Other than violence breaking out at the food distribution trucks, I haven't seen any *rampaging domestic terrorists*. It's people sharing your ideology that are keeping us locked away in our homes and afraid of our own shadows when we should be living our lives."

Jack's words caught Crestwater off guard. He'd thought Jack was surrendering to mainstream thought. "Your reaction tells me I misjudged you and you're not to be trusted."

Jack silently admonished himself for the slip and attempted to recover. "Ha, just testing you, Agent Crestwater. Our leaders *should* be in DC."

Crestwater regarded Jack through squinted eyes, heavy with distrust. And he realized he'd enjoy breaking his news. "Jack, with our final shipment delivering this afternoon, it's time we discuss Stinger Machinery's go-forward plan."

Sweat ran down Jack's back. "I'm interested to hear your plan. How will Stinger Machinery be supporting our government in the future?"

Agent Crestwater stood and motioned for Jack to follow him to his office. As he moved to take a seat, Jack's eyes scanned his desk, coming to rest on a brightly colored children's book. Jack went rigid when the title became visible: *My First Book of Sign Language.*

Agent Crestwater sat, then quickly covered the book with a manila folder. "Jack, about our go-forward plan. The government has determined it's a wise move to assume ownership of Stinger Machinery. Actually, all U.S. manufacturing will be assimilated into the newly formed Bureau of Responsible Manufacturing. During our partnerships with various manufacturers, we've learned that if left to your own devices, you will run yourselves out of business. And while racing to the bottom, you'll destroy our planet. Simply unacceptable."

Jack's head tilted in question. "You're nationalizing my family's business? Is that what's happening? Taking everything I've built?"

Agent Crestwater nodded his head and feigned empathy. "I realize this must be difficult to hear, Jack. That for all these years, you've been running your family's business into the ground while accelerating the planet's demise. But your government is here to help right the ship. We'll employ you as a manager, at a reduced salary of course, but at least you'll be employed. We'll still need to address the matter of your government loan, obviously. However, I'm confident a compromise can be reached."

"You, your government, silenced me. Took everything from me. I'm losing my home, my life savings, my wife, all of it. And you're blaming me. You're telling me it's all my fault?"

Crestwater shifted in his chair before responding. "Yes, what's happening to your business and businesses across the country is both a direct and indirect result of your actions, your way of life…"

"Shut the fuck up, Crestwater. I swear to Christ I'll rip your throat out if you utter another syllable." Jack took a menacing step in Crestwater's direction, causing the man to flinch. "This was the plan from day one. This has nothing to do with my book or beliefs. You never intended to remove your talons from Stinger Machinery. Your plan was to nationalize every business in the country. Turn us into government servants. COMPLETE CONTROL."

Jack snaked around the desk, intent on ending Crestwater, when a hand grasped his shoulder and spun him. Blinded by rage, his fist arced towards his assailant on instinct. His mind registered Armin's face after it dropped from view, narrowly avoiding Jack's blow.

"Whoa, Jack. Calm down!" Armin yelled.

Jack's mind struggled to regain control. He felt as if he'd been jolted from a dream. "Armin, I'm sorry. I'm so sorry. I didn't mean... man, I just lost control."

Armin unfolded from his crouch and locked Jack in a hard stare. "I'm not sure what was happening in here. But we need you in the shop. It's an emergency."

Jack nodded as his body trembled, bleeding off the adrenalin that had flooded his system. "Yeah, it's, ah, it's an emergency. Let's go," he said, just above a whisper.

"You're lucky your friend interrupted, *Mister* Stinger. I shudder to think the heft of my response had you followed through on your Neanderthal-ish actions. Weren't you granted non-essential visitation rights? Be a shame if they were revoked, don't you agree?"

Jack straightened at Agent Crestwater's words. "Yes, Agent Crestwater, it would be a shame." His back still to the BHR agent, he took a deep calming breath before continuing. "Sorry about my outburst. I assure you it won't happen again."

He swallowed the bile stinging his throat and on unsteady legs followed Armin from the office.

"Oh, and Jack, I'll have the transfer of ownership paperwork ready for your signature tomorrow, first thing. It's our new way forward, Jack. Very exciting times."

Jack stopped at the office threshold, and over his shoulder, said, "I'm looking forward to it, Agent Crestwater. Very exciting indeed."

***

"What the hell was that?" UW signed. "You nearly got yourself arrested. If Armin hadn't overheard your conversation and stopped you, you'd be on your way to jail."

Still fighting to sort out his emotions, Jack signed, "They're taking the business. Nationalizing it."

UW, Randy, Armin, and Jack stood huddled around the CNC machine, pretending to be performing an inspection. "We figured something like this would happen, Jack," UW began. "Now, keep your anger in check. We can't afford to have you in jail." His sign language reflected his anger, and Jack understood why.

He prepared to respond when movement to his left caught his attention. One of the BHR machinists was floating around the shop, attempting to gain a better view of them. "Can I help you with something?" Jack barked.

Startled, the man shook his head and scurried into the office area. "I know where he's going. And it isn't good. Crestwater has a book of sign language on his desk."

"Shit, shit, shit," Randy signed animatedly.

"Let's finish this at my house, tonight. Randy, Armin, we'll fill you in later. Now, break something on this machine," UW ordered.

With a huge grin, Randy pulled the digital monitor from its mount and dropped it a flash before Crestwater stormed into the shop.

"Agent Crestwater," Jack began, a grin tugging at his own mouth. "This machine will be offline for the foreseeable future."

Crestwater, ever wary of entering the shop area, locked Jack in a derisive glare from where he stood. "FIX IT! We've received our next project. One I'm sure you'll approve of."

CHAPTER 43

WILLIS STINGER'S HOME

Jack's excitement was helping him stuff the day's events. In twenty minutes, he would see Lisa for the first time in months. Hell, he couldn't even remember the last time he'd talked to her. The only updates UW would give him were "She's safe and busy." Busy doing what remained to be seen.

He slapped his Nonessential Visitation Pass on the dashboard, as the Bureau of Civic Responsibility's directions mandated, and pulled from his garage. As he exited his drive, the daily food distribution truck was pulling to a stop at the end of the street.

The gaunt stress-weary faces of his neighbors already standing in line rushed past his passenger side window. The scene stirred his anger. They were defeated, the government rendering them dependent subjects, reliant on the bureaucracy for every aspect of life.

A blaring horn pulled his attention back to the road in front of him. He slammed to a stop mere feet from the food distribution truck's grill, which had pulled into a blocking position in the middle of the intersection.

Jack raised his hands in the universal driver-code asking the other driver, "What the hell."

Two armed men, clad in black, burst from the cab and quickly approached his Yukon. Jack realized he was their target and placed his hands on the dashboard, hoping to avoid being shot by an overzealous BHR agent.

Standing at the grill of his Yukon, a tall heavily muscled agent hollered, "Hands out the window. Open your door using the outside handle. Exit slowly, keeping your hands above your head."

Stunned, Jack hesitated, angering the agent.

"Now," he screamed as he brought his MP5 to high-ready position. "This doesn't need to end badly."

Shocked by the threat, Jack followed the agent's orders and quickly exited.

"Keep your eyes on me. Why are you driving after work hours? I don't see an unrestricted person pass."

"My 85NEV pass is on the dashboard. I-I'm not breaking any laws," Jack stuttered.

"Smith, retrieve the civilian's pass," the agent ordered the second agent. "Civilian, take two steps in my direction."

"How about you lower that gun," Jack asked as he took the requested steps. "I'm not a threat."

Smith entered Jack's SUV through the passenger door, quickly retrieving the pass. "Looks legit, Samson. I'll call in the authorization code."

Jack's knees buckled when he remembered his sat-phone sitting in the center console storage compartment. The console Agent Smith was currently resting his arm on while verifying the authenticity of Jack's pass.

He turned his head, searching for an escape route should things bounce sideways, and found a wall of humanity enthralled by the quickly unfolding drama. "Keep your eyes on the agent.

Like he ordered you." The angry voice traveled from somewhere deep in the crowd as others nodded in agreement.

That's some unsettling shit, Jack thought. And realized the agents wouldn't have to shoot him if he ran. The crowd would stop him. They needed to eat, to live. And if turning on him meant getting a few extra morsels added to their handout, so be it.

A snicker from Samson pulled Jack's attention back to the front of the truck. "Remember that just in case you ever decide to act up. We have eyes everywhere."

"Got no reason to *act up*," Jack answered. "I'm a well-behaved citizen. But I'd like to lower my hands; my arms are feeling like pins and needles."

In an over-the-top response aimed to demonstrate his power over Jack to the crowd, Samson took a hard step in Jack's direction. "I'll tell you when you can put your arms down. And now isn't *when*." He grinned as the crowd cheered him on. His power was now absolute.

"Hey," Smith yelled from inside Jack's truck, forcing his heart to skip in his chest. "He's clear. Pass checks out."

"You can lower your hands. But don't move," Samson began. "Smith, move the truck and start feeding these good people. This *civilian* wasted enough of their time."

"I did nothing wrong, asshole," Jack whispered as he rubbed blood back into his hands.

Samson moved faster than Jack thought possible for a man his size. "Do you have something to say?" he barked, now standing nose to nose with Jack. "Please, share your thoughts with me. Or you could call our complaint department at 1-800-Shut Up."

Jack cracked his neck like a prizefighter as he glared at the agent. He'd put men like Samson down a hundred times in his life. "I'll be sure to call and compliment you. Your service was outstanding."

"That's what I figured. Have a wonderful day." Samson faced the crowd and bellowed, "Who's ready for dinner?"

***

Jack jumped from his Yukon so quickly he had to lean back in to make sure he'd actually placed it in Park. After confirming he had, he bolted towards the door to his uncle's home. As he jogged up the walkway, he found UW staring at him with his patented disapproving glare.

"What'd I do?" he signed, slowing his stride and cognizant of the 85 Plumbing truck still parked on the street.

"You're late. You should have been here twenty minutes ago. I pictured you sitting in a government Gulag."

Jack joined his uncle on the porch and gave a crooked smile. "Well, I had a run-in with a food truck. I ordered a taco which seemed to make the cooks really mad."

"Yeah, that's what I figured," UW chuckled while signing. "Well, get in the house. *Dinner* is waiting. But, before you do, wave to the nice agents in the van. We don't want to appear rude."

Jack and UW turned towards the van and gave vigorous waves accompanied by toothy grins, then pushed through the door.

Jack pulled to a stop three steps into his uncle's home. He'd expected Lisa to greet him the moment he stepped over the threshold. But the house appeared empty.

"Where's my wife?" he asked.

UW craned his neck towards the large picture window, ensuring the blinds were closed. "We have to be more careful. With Crestwater studying sign language, it's safe to assume the agents in the van are too. So, going forward, we only speak when we are certain no one's watching."

Jack nodded, the gravity of what he'd seen on Crestwater's desk weighing heavy on his mind. They'd overlooked the zeal displayed by the Bureau of Harm Reduction to achieve complete control. Something they'd need to address.

"Follow me," UW said as he headed towards the basement stairs.

His excitement building to childlike levels, Jack was crushed when he entered the basement and found it empty.

"UW, I'm in no mood for games."

His uncle smiled and walked to the bookshelves flanking the basement to the left. Jack watched, impatiently, as UW pulled a book from the shelf, reached his hand into the cavity its removal created, and eased a small section of dark wood away, exposing a numbered keypad.

A secondhand tick later, the enormous section of bookshelf was sliding to the right. Jack's astonishment turned to jubilance as his wife's smiling face appeared. She was seated at a desk piled high with legal pads and electronic equipment the likes of which Jack had never seen.

"You're late," she signed as a smile tugged at her lips.

Struggling to contain his emotions, and reminding himself not to speak, he rushed to embrace Lisa. Pulling her to her feet, he stared into her eyes, then wrapped her in his arms. His jaw hinged open to tell her how much he'd missed her, then slammed shut, remembering the BHR was listening.

Lost in the moment, he jumped when his uncle said aloud, "Get a room, you two."

Jack pulled away from Lisa and glared at his uncle. "What the hell are you doing?" he signed. "The BHR is listening."

"Oh, they're listening, but they can't hear us," UW said, gesturing to the sealed entrance. "Walls are poured concrete, a foot thick. Entrance is two inches of steel covered by an inch of mahogany. Ceiling is lined with ATS acoustic panels over more concrete. We're safe."

Jack stood silent, taking in the information. His uncle had been a step ahead his entire life, and this room proved it. "Well, this explains why your basement felt so claustrophobic during our meeting last spring."

UW's expectant stare prompted Jack to look a question at him. "Damn, Jack, look around. You're taking the fun out of it," his uncle practically shouted while sweeping his hands around.

Jack's eyes followed the direction his uncle indicated. His mouth gaped in disbelief when the area's scope came into view. He'd been so preoccupied with Lisa, he'd completely ignored his surroundings.

"What in the actual hell?" he mumbled.

"Impressive, isn't it?" Lisa said as she slipped under his arm.

Still in shock, Jack nodded as he scanned the room. The walls were lined, top to bottom, with hundreds of what appeared to be military-grade weapons. Some styles he recognized, others he'd never seen. The collective size of the arsenal filled the air with the syrupy tang of gun oil and cleaning solvent. Crates containing items unknown were stacked floor to ceiling at the far end flanked by equally high stacks of metal ammo cans.

"What's in the crates?" Jack asked, eyes still investigating.

"Food, freeze-dried food. And water. Enough to feed six for a year," UW proclaimed proudly. "No MREs; those things are nasty and have a shorter shelf life."

Jack's eyes fell on a folding bed, the type used in hotels, set in the middle of the room. "And this is where you've been living for the entire summer?"

"Late winter, spring, summer, and now heading into fall," Lisa answered. "Showers and bathroom breaks take a bit of coordinating. But we make it work."

Jack caught the phrasing. "Bathroom breaks? Sounds like you're in grade school. What the hell are you doing all day?"

Lisa slid her arm along Jack's lower back and used it as leverage to spin him slowly towards where he'd found her sitting a moment ago. "I work all day, Jack."

Facing the empty chair he'd found her in, his eyes drifted to the desk supporting several large radios and an open laptop. Her sat-phone to the side connected to a charging cord buzzed with an incoming call which she ignored.

"Lisa?"

"I've been talking to a lot of people, Jack. A lot of very angry people."

CHAPTER 44

MOUNT WEATHER

Chief of Staff Roberts walked a circle in Mount Weather's Situation Room, awaiting Rosos' return call. Today promised to be momentous, the day he'd been waiting for. But it had arrived sooner than planned and in a manner he was unprepared for. Something felt... off.

His personal phone buzzing interrupted his third trip around the room. "Mister Rosos, thank you for returning my call," he said. "Everything is in place. However, I have a question."

"For the love of God, what now?"

Roberts flinched at Rosos' sharp tone, reminding him of how their relationship had deteriorated since Zhang Bu had joined their *team*. "Sir, do we need to employ such drastic measures? We've virtually guaranteed our victory at the polls. We have only two weeks until the midterms. Can't we wait till then? This action seems... excessive."

A man, he assumed to be Zhang, began yelling in Mandarin. When he finished, Roberts addressed the outburst in an even tone. "Mister Zhang, I didn't realize you were joining us. To address your request, *this fool will not shut up.* If you'd like to finish our conversation in your native tongue, we can. I assure you I'm quite fluent in Mandarin."

Rosos' chuckle felt reassuring; Roberts still held a place in his keeper's hierarchy.

"Mister Roberts. I believe you have insulted our friend, Mister Zhang. This pleases me. I had begun to worry you had lost your edge." Rosos' thick accent, coupled with his use of a speakerphone, made it nearly impossible to understand him. "Now, to answer your question. I don't care if you feel our actions to be excessive."

"Yes, I understand," Roberts responded quietly. "But I do prefer we follow our original plan."

"A moment ago you said you've *virtually guaranteed* our victory. Do you know what *virtually* means?" Rosos interrupted. "It means almost, near, practically, or any number of adverbs which indicate the possibility of failure. My plan changes the adverb to absolutely. Now would you rather have absolute power or virtually absolute power?"

Roberts held his tongue; his hands were already drenched in the blood of dozens of innocent people. What harm would he suffer by adding a few more drops? "Absolute power, of course. It's settled. Genus will join the joint session of Congress at seven via video. The session will begin after Genus delivers her remarks. All proceedings will be televised, as you requested."

"Mister Roberts, we're on the cusp of the new way forward. Our new world order, so to speak. And you have secured your position in history, the right side of history." Rosos sounded like a coach, inspiring his team to push past the pain as victory was at their fingertips. "We are changing the world for humanity's betterment. Your name will be forever associated with this glorious event!"

Roberts' chest swelled. "The right side of history, sir. A history which shall pave the way to unity, equality, and opportunity for the loyal among us." His inflection neared evangelical status.

Rosos' smile evident as he spoke, he said, "You have much to do. I'll let you tend to your duties. Good day."

Roberts stood awestruck, perched on the edge of greatness. He would not fail. He glanced at his to-do list and dialed the number for his head of security. "Yes, Jeffery, please remove your guards from the lower levels of the Capitol building. The security detail guarding the intersection of First Street North East and East Capitol Street North East needs reinforcement. We've received INTEL of an attempted incursion from that direction."

***

"Hello America, how are you? Oh, I love that song, and I love all of you. You've been so brave during these troublesome times. I'm so very proud of every one of you. Kisses all around."

"Follow the Goddamn script, Genus," Roberts shouted into her headset.

Covering the microphone, he turned to face a second monitor broadcasting from Raven Rock. "How much medication has she taken?"

"Not enough to make her act like an imbecile," answered Genus' personal physician.

"Whoop, whoop, to Arlo Guthrie. Am I right?"

"Oh Jesus Christ, follow the script. Or I will have you executed on live television."

Her reaction told Roberts she heard him, and more importantly, understood. Her transition from court jester to head of state was jarring as she suddenly went serious and stared into the camera. "Enough of my levity. I'm here today to show you, all of America, and indeed the world, that we stand unified. We are strong as we face adversity together. And that your government is working for you, the American people."

Roberts exhaled as his hope that they might make it through this grew. His respite was fleeting as Genus suddenly appeared confused.

Her face scrunched as she tilted her head in question. "Whaaat does that say?" she slurred. "Oh, I got it now. I'm sure you're concerned about our brave and fearless President Eden's health. Rest easy knowing your government has recruited the brightest minds in medicine to care for him. Sadly, I must report, his condition has not improved. But they have stabilized him, and he is comfortable as his doctors continue their work to discover the cause of his mysterious illness."

Genus fell silent as her eyes followed the teleprompter and her mouth moved as if she was reading the words to herself.

"Vice President Genus," Roberts said while pinching the bridge of his nose. "The words on the teleprompter are to be spoken aloud. They're not for your personal enjoyment."

"Please rewind the prompter," Genus asked, clearly startled back to the moment by Roberts. "As our dear President fights a valiant war to recover, the role of President falls on my strong shoulders. I assure you, your safety during these troublesome times is my top priority. A responsibility I take seriously. However, to aid our government's efforts in securing a safe America for all, we have initiated several measures. If determined necessary, our citizen soldiers, a loyal group of everyday citizens, will be granted full policing authority. We hope that their services are never needed. But it feels safe knowing we can call them into action on a moment's notice."

Genus paused as her announcement created a stir amongst the Congressmen and women gathered in the House Chamber. "I thought we had notified you all," she proffered. "Didn't you receive an advanced copy of my remarks?"

Roberts, unaware a two-way audio feed had been established between Raven Rock and the House Chamber, came unglued at the revelation. "Cut the House audio feed, NOW. Who the fuck authorized it? NOT IMPORTANT. Genus' feed is video only; correct this situation, NOW!"

Roberts' harsh tone sent the AV staff into a frenzy of keyboard strokes and verbal commands. Genus' confused look confirmed the audio had been severed.

"Genus, continue with your remarks," Roberts roared, reaching the end of his patience.

She jumped at Roberts' scorching voice in her earpiece before resuming. "Um, as I was saying. With the addition of the citizen soldiers, we are prepared for any catastrophic event or attack the domestic terrorists have planned. It is also important to note that until such time as we've beaten back the assault on our freedom, certain liberties we all enjoy must be suspended. A full list can be found at WhiteHouse dot gov. If we have not granted you internet privileges, a hard-copy list will be mailed to you by the Bureaus of Harm Reduction and Civic Responsibility. As we enter the dark winter ahead, we have lifted the weight of consent from your already overburdened shoulders. Going forward, our country will run on the premise of consent of the government. No longer will you be forced to struggle beneath the yoke of being asked permission for your government to act.

We have abolished the term "consent of the governed," freeing you to focus on living your best life."

***

Acting Speaker of The House Mary Barnet sensed Genus' remarks coming to an end. Still, she hesitated to call the joint session to order. The Vice President's well-established erratic behavior when speaking publicly kept her planted firmly in her seat.

As Genus droned on, Barnet's gaze slid around the perimeter of the sacred House Chamber. Hundreds of security personnel stood ready in the shadows cast against the dark wood paneling. The approach to the House Chamber had been cordoned off with steel barricades standing over seven feet high. Each of the news crews was subjected to intense vetting and assigned an armed escort. She had personally presided over the placement of guards in the lower levels of the Capitol building, ensuring it had been sealed tight. Their safety had been guaranteed, a guarantee she felt Eden's chief of staff had honored. She despised the troll. But he had been true to his word.

As she searched the worried faces of her colleagues, she felt a surge of pride that they had put aside their political differences to unite for the American people. As a smile creased her features, her name was suddenly blaring over the Chamber's speakers.

"Hello, Speaker Barnet, are you listening?" Genus' cackling laughter followed her question.

Barnet sprang to her feet and snatched the gavel from the podium. "Before calling our momentous joint session to order, I want to take this opportunity to remind the American public that your ballots for the midterm elections, less than two weeks from today, have been mailed to your resident dwelling. After completing them, return them to the Bureau of Harm Reduction postmarked no later than November the second."

Her smile beamed as she stood proudly at the Speaker of The House's podium. "Ladies and gentlemen. I now call this joint session of Congress to order."

As her gavel arced toward the block, she noticed the wire protruding from its side for the first time. Her eyes widened in horror. As the gavel struck the hardwood sound-block, she registered the click of a pressure switch. Her warning cry caught in her throat as she felt the rumbling in the soles of her feet. Its intensity grew as the muffled sound of four hundred pounds of C4 strapped to the building's support beams received its orders to detonate deep within the bowels of the Capitol Building.

The panic-stricken cries of her colleagues were silenced as gouts of reddish-orange flames, tinged black at their edges, burst from the floor. Clinging to hope, she fled the podium for the nearest exit, only to be engulfed by flames as a secondary round of explosions ripped through the aisle and the floor crumbled, sending her to the inferno below.

Roberts' feed cut off as the second round of explosions pulverized the House Chamber and spread throughout the Capitol Complex. A smile tugged at his lips. Washington was burning.

This book is a departure from my other books, and I hope you enjoyed it. My intent was to bring the same humour found in the Divided America Zombie Apocalypse series, but as I wrote I saw hints of the story playing out in everyday life. The result was a more serious tone, one which I hope we never see as reality.

Next From B.D. Lutz

Citizen Soldier: Book Two of The Consent Of The Governed Series

Other Books From B.D. Lutz

The Divided America Zombie Apocalypse Series

Divided We Fell

Of Patriots And Tyrants

A Dangerous Freedom

Eternal Vigilance

Reviews are valuable to independent writers. Please consider leaving yours where you purchased this book.

Feel free to like me on Facebook at B.D. Lutz/Author Page. You'll be the first notified of specials and new releases. You can email me at: CLELUTZ11@gmail.com. I'd love to hear from you.

ABOUT THE AUTHOR

I was born in Cleveland, Ohio. I now live in NEO (North East Ohio) with my wonderful wife (she told me to say that). We recently became grandparent (young grandparents, mind you). That little angel is the apple of our eyes.

In my early adult life, I spent time as a Repo-Man for a rent-to-own furniture company and bill collector. Then I decided that was a tough way to earn a living and spent twenty-seven years working my way through sales management in corporate America. I've always wanted to write books, and I realized that we, you and me, have about fifteen minutes on the face of this planet and I needed to do one of the things I had always wanted to do. And, well, this is it.

If you're wondering, yes, I'm a conservative, I own guns, and I hate paying taxes.

Made in the USA
Columbia, SC
27 August 2022

65532480R00148